BORDER GUNS

BORDER GUNS

EUGENE CUNNINGHAM

THORNDIKE
CHIVERS

This Large Print edition is published by Thorndike Press, Waterville, Maine, USA and by BBC Audiobooks Ltd, Bath, England.

Thorndike Press, a part of Gale, Cengage Learning.

A different version of this story was first published in **Lariat Story Magazine** under the title BUCK FROM THE BORDER.

The text of this Large Print edition is unabridged.

Other aspects of the book may vary from the original edition.

Set in 16 pt. Plantin.

Printed on permanent paper.

LIBRARY OF CONGRESS CATALOGING-IN-PUBLICATION DATA

Cunningham, Eugene, 1896–1957.
  Border guns / by Eugene Cunningham.
    p. cm. — (Thorndike Press large print western)
  "A different version of this story was first published in Lariat Story Magazine under the title Buck from the border."
    ISBN-13: 978-1-4104-0911-9 (hardcover : alk. paper)
    ISBN-10: 1-4104-0911-2 (hardcover : alk. paper)
    1. Large type books. I. Title.
  PS3505.U428B67 2008
  813'.54—dc22   2008021510

BRITISH LIBRARY CATALOGUING-IN-PUBLICATION DATA AVAILABLE

Published in 2008 in the U.S. by arrangement with Golden West Literary Agency.

Published in 2009 in the U.K. by arrangement with Golden West Literary Agency.

U.K. Hardcover: 978 1 408 41293 0 (Chivers Large Print)
U.K. Softcover: 978 1 408 41294 7 (Camden Large Print)

Printed in the United States of America
1 2 3 4 5 6 7 12 11 10 09 08

BORDER GUNS

CHAPTER ONE

An ancient trail looped across the yellow sand of the flat desert. It curled like a rattlesnake between the dull green greasewood bushes, the thorny mesquite and dagger-leaved yuccas. It rose gradually, to scale the rugged, barren foothills of the Caballos.

Moccasined feet had pounded it, and the bare hoofs of shaggy ponies ridden by Apache, Comanche and Lipan. Away and away south, in the green and treacherous wildernesses that edge the Rio Grande, still the old trail showed. There it forded the wide river between sucking quicksands, to lead on to the gray-brown adobe towns of the Mexicans.

Ross Varney had followed it, now, for many years, straight from the Rio Grande. But the long-limbed black he sat so gracefully showed little trace of journeying. He had more than once covered his sixty miles at almost a steady gallop, between sun and sun, and this time Ross had not ridden him hard. For he had a particular errand, Ross did. He would reach his destination without having to kill the best horse he had ever seen.

"Rayo ought to be right over the hills," he drawled aloud. "Right over yonder."

Abruptly he fell silent, with clark blue eyes narrowing, lighted by the inner fire of his thoughts. The black horse, plains-bred though he was, climbed the lifting trail with easy surging of great haunch muscles. Ross Varney sat with seeming negligence, but alert for anything that might move among the scrub-oaks and junipers ahead.

He was something under six feet, lean of body, wide of shoulder. He gave easily to the black's motion, the horseman born, and dressed the part in wide-rimmed black Stetson set upon yellow hair, shirt of blue flannel, gray jeans trousers tucked neatly into bootlegs. Always his hands brushed lightly the smooth walnut stocks of the two long-barreled Colts that swung cannily low, the toes of their holsters held down by thongs around his thighs.

His roving eyes found something presently. There was a little rocky space beside the trail, fifteen or twenty feet across. Upon a flat rock in its center a ropy coil was moveless. Ross Varney's blue eyes twinkled. He flipped a shell from his belt. Up from that coil came a flat, triangular head. It began to sway rhythmically back and forth. Then Ross set in the hooks. The black leaped into a gallop in a stride.

Twenty yards he covered at a racing gallop. They came alongside the rattler. Ross could hear that sinister rustling, like dry leaves in a petty tempest. They passed it. Ross whirled in the big saddle, his right hand flashed diagonally across his front, and out came the left-side Colt. At the tail of its motion the gun barked and that vicious head was smashed. Ross grinned — not exactly like one pleased with a surprising feat of marksmanship, but with a slow, somehow sinister lip-widening, that held a threat.

"Beautiful!" remarked a voice above and to the right of him, as he reined the black in again to an effortless running walk.

Ross was taken utterly by surprise. The black sat down upon his tail as the bridle reins tightened convulsively. Ross glared up in the direction of the voice, the not yet holstered Colt lifting instinctively. Then, scowling blankly, he lowered his hand and the gun slid back into its scabbard.

Upon a little rise of the hillside a slim girl sat a smallish brown horse, hands comfortably upon saddle horn. Evidently she had just pushed her mount through a screen of brush. Evidently, also, she had witnessed Ross's bit of gunplay. Half her smile betokened admiration, but half, Ross thought, mirrored a secret amusement — like that of a grown-up who stumbles upon a youngster playing pirate.

"Was it — an accident?" she asked, wide brown eyes steady upon him, still smiling.

Then Ross smiled back at her.

"Accident?" he repeated. "Why, you surely don't think anybody could do that on purpose?"

But to himself he was breathing, "Pretty! *Por dios! Por dios!* Pretty! Wonder who she can be?"

"Why" — the girl was studying him intently and now the smile was gone, as if she thought of other, more serious, things — "there are men in Rayo and around it who could do that shooting. Who could do it — oh, twice out of three times, perhaps."

"You don't mean it!" Ross cried, widening his eyes innocently. "My goodness! What kind of a country is this, anyhow? I hope these gentlemen you're mentioning don't act vicious to strangers! Maybe I'd better not go to Rayo at all."

She merely watched him for a long moment, the small oval of her face grave. Then abruptly she ticked the brown horse and came down the slope to Ross. Nearer view of her made Ross's already speeded pulses hammer faster. At twenty-five, he was a young man of wide and harsh experiences, many of which he would never mention. But, staring at her, somehow he knew that he had blundered into a meeting that was going to affect his whole life. For he had met the girl who made something in him cry out, "You're a one-woman *hombre,* Ross Varney — and this is the woman."

"Perhaps you would be wise to turn aside from Rayo!" she said suddenly. "I'm sure I don't know what's there to attract an honest man. And I've known the town since it was nothing but a couple of trading stores, before the mines were opened and the gunmen came."

"But a fellow goes traveling to kind of educate himself," ventured Ross with straight face. "To see different places and different kinds of people, you know. Maybe I'd better go to Rayo, after all. Just to say I've been there."

"Then I'll ride part way with you," she shrugged, pushing the brown forward. "It's

11

six or seven miles farther. I turn off before we get to Rayo."

"You don't live in town?" Ross inquired. This girl was not going to get out of his sight, if he could help it, without his finding out more about her. "I'm Ross Varney, cowpunch. Last place I wandered around was the Rio Grande country."

"From the Border," she nodded, with interest. "No, I don't live in town. I live with my uncle, Yocum Nowle, on the N-Bar. He's an old-timer here."

She seemed to be thinking of something else. Ross stole a covert glance at the left hand that held her bridle reins. It was wholly ringless — a small discovery that meant much to him.

"It's a lonesome sort of trail you came, up from the Rio Grande?" she said presently.

"No-o, not exactly. Plenty of folks on it farther south. Haven't met anybody today, though."

"Nobody? Nobody at all?" she demanded tensely.

Ross's brows climbed. He shook his head. "Nobody at all."

The ivory of her face had gone red and pale in flashing succession. Now it seemed to resume a natural color; her expression, too, lost its gravity. She faced him with

12

twinkle in brown eyes, red lips curving faintly. "Then perhaps we won't have any more ferocious citizens arriving today."

But he knew that this was not the reason behind her urgent question. She had been fearing to find someone on this trail, and it relieved her tremendously to find herself wrong in the expectation. Ross wondered, but after a time he mentally shrugged his shoulders.

"What's wrong with Rayo?" he asked. "No honest folks in it — or around it?"

"Around it, yes. In it — oh, there are honest people, of course. But they are in such a minority and are so preyed upon by tinhorn gamblers and thieves of one variety or another that they hardly count."

"Town officers? County officers? How about them?"

"Sheriff Troop is an honest man and an old-timer, but he seems helpless. The city marshal, Lake Ellard, is a killer from up the trail somewhere. It is his creatures — old friends and new — who commit most of the crimes. The only thing one can say for Ellard is that he does enforce with an iron hand such regulations as he makes. For instance, nobody is permitted to fire a gun within town limits. The penalty is arrest and a heavy fine. To resist arrest by the slightest gesture means death. Ellard is deadly!"

"Bet the cowboys don't care a whole lot for the marshal." Ross grinned reminiscently. "No more shooting up the village, huh?"

"Absolutely not! But that's not the whole secret of their hatred for Ellard. His gang of towners dislike the range folk, so life is made generally miserable for a cowboy in town. So they back Sheriff Troop. But — and this complicates matters further — Marshal Ellard has made enemies among some of the prominents of the old cow-rustlers and all-around criminals. They weren't strong enough to buck him openly, so they moved over to Rawles, above the mines. They are avowed supporters of Sheriff Troop, but still criminals. That's embarrassing."

"Matt Sayer the worst man around here?" Ross asked. His tone was casual, but he had to keep a strong grip on himself as he voiced the name of the man he intended to kill on sight.

"Sayer?" she frowned. "I don't think there's any such man here."

"Oh, yes! Must be. Quite a killer, I heard down the line. They said he was up in Rayo. Lightning gunman."

"I never heard of him," she said.

They rode on silently until a side-road opened from the Rayo trail. Here the girl reined in the brown horse and sat for a moment regarding Ross with a faint smile upon her lips — but with brown eyes very serious.

"This is the N-Bar road, Mr. Varney," she said. "You'll be in Rayo in a very few minutes and — I trust that you'll enjoy your stay there. But I'm afraid you're going to be disappointed about Matt Sayer. I'm sure no such man has ever been in the camp. But, if you ask about him there, keep your eyes down. You might possibly fool a man — some men — but any woman can read your eyes. . . . Good-by, Mr. Cowboy on the War Trail!"

She whirled the brown horse up the ranch road and was out of sight between the rows of scrubby trees before Ross could speak. He sat dumbly staring after her. He was going to find out all about her, *he* was! And now, he knew precisely one fact about her — the relationship to Yocum Nowle. But she had read *him* like coarse print; had read the killing lust in his eyes when he mentioned the name of the killer of Baldy Fay. . . .

But as he saw Rayo sprawling among the cottonwoods ahead of him, he grinned slowly to himself and jogged onward. Her name might be Mary or Jane or anything you liked to guess. No matter — he had met her and had seen the sort of girl he had never expected to find. That was a good big day's work by itself.

"Just as soon as I hang this Sayer skunk's hide on my corral fence, I'm surely going to camp on one girl's trail," he told himself quietly. " 'Was the shot an accident?' she said. *Dios à dios à dios!* I wonder — I wonder if a fellow could start all over again, this far away from his home country? Wonder if a fellow could put the tale into words that a girl like that could understand?"

And, remembering the clear brown eyes, the honest directness of their gaze, a cold fear went riding with him down the crowded single street of Rayo — which was known, just then, as the roughest, hardest town in the whole West. Worse, even, than old Dodge City during the roaring days of the trail herds.

Over the Caballos the sun was dropping. The plank sidewalks of Rayo were like the bare space about an anthill. Cowboys rolled along awkwardly on high heels; dance-hall girls, berouged, bedizened, shrill of voice and laughter, moved on the arms of their escorts of the moment — burly miners,

16

sleek, cold-eyed gamblers, or roughly dressed bull-whackers. Pianos tinkled tinnily from within the long adobe buildings that housed saloon and dance-hall and gambling hell.

Ross was no stranger to this sort of town. El Paso he knew quite well, and many another, but here was a town the brazen gaiety of which outdid even the border towns where slowly, but steadily, the respectables were gaining the upper hand.

He pushed the black forward, looking for livery corral or hotel sign. He was nearing the long sweep of the Swan Saloon when there sounded a sudden splatter of shots and out through a swinging door a man came backing, a grizzled man with seamed brown face and drooping gray mustache, who held at waist-level in each hand a smoke-wreathed Colt.

Out across the wooden gallery backed this figure, for all the world like a grim old wolf, shooting as he came, right hand, left hand. A man appeared in the doorway, to go sprawling upon his face, body seeming all joints as he fell. Came a shot from within the dusky saloon. The old man crumpled, guns dropping from his gnarled hands. He had been shot squarely through the face.

Ross had reined in with first sound of the

affray. The sidewalks had been magically cleared so that the duel had been carried on in a deserted open space. Now Ross waited, staring in quick alternation from the dead man in the street to the saloon door. Appeared now a man of middle height and pale, square face, with the iciest pair of gray eyes Ross had ever seen in human head. He was immaculately dressed, with fine black woolen trousers pulled down carefully over polished boots. The twin Colts in his hands were gold- and silver-plated, pearl-handled.

Slowly this man advanced across the wooden gallery, those ice-colored eyes seeming to watch not only the still figure ahead, but all that went on to right and left. Straight out to the dead man he went, and stirred him callously with a boot-toe. Then he turned back toward the sidewalk and in turning revealed to Ross a large gold shield pinned to the lapel of his frock coat. Ross read the legend on it: *City Marshal.*

"Well, our late sheriff's been asking for that a long time," he drawled.

More men came from the saloon. They picked up both bodies — that of the grim-faced old man, whom Ross guessed to be the sheriff, and the handsome, Mexican-brown gunman whom Troop had killed in the doorway. They carried them inside and

Ross, slipping down and knotting his bridle-reins to the hitch-rack, followed.

"This Troop surely was a wolf!" he thought, with sight of two more bodies lying in the back and surrounded by men who obviously were of the marshal's party. "When he went out, he passed through smoke and sent three ahead of him! Sorry I didn't get to know him."

Chapter Two

He attracted no attention as he stood at the bar — or so it seemed. But presently, as he moved his second drink in aimless figures upon the mahogany bar, the icy-eyed man with the marshal's shield came through the crowd and moved straight down upon Ross, who made no pretense of not seeing his approach.

So they faced each other while the crowd, seeming to sense something tense in Lake Ellard's regard of a stranger, watched silently, almost breathlessly. And Ellard looked up a little into Ross Varney's dark blue eyes, his face changeless as he stared.

"I'm Ellard, City Marshal," he said quietly, in the same low drawl which had voiced his epitaph for Sheriff Troop a few minutes before.

"You can call me Varney," Ross responded when Ellard seemed to wait.

"Drifting through?" Ellard probed. Ross shrugged.

"*Quién sabe? Quién sabe?* Never worry about things like that till I'm broke — and I'm not broke yet."

"Texas man, huh?" But it was a statement, not a query. "Saw your rig — and your rope — a spell back."

"Well, if I'm not Texas, I reckon I'll do till one comes along." Ross grinned — but only with his lips. His eyes were duskiest violet, right now. "And you? Where are you from?"

The pale, square, clean-shaven face hardened until the tense muscles of cheeks were like gray marble. But that was the only change of expression perceptible. As for Ross, he still wore the faint, mocking grin with which he had flung his question insolently in the marshal's face. There was moving deep within him a lift like that which lay in the third drink of an evening. In a moment, it might be, he and this pallid killer would be matching speed on the draw.

"Fellow" — the marshal's drawl had dropped a full note until it was hardly more than a whisper, a deadly whisper — "I'm Lake Ellard. I'm City Marshal of Rayo. And where I come from ain't of no meaning at all. I'm here! That's what signifies to you!"

"Thanks!" Ross grinned. "We certainly figure just alike, don't we? We're here and the only thing that matters is what we do here, *es verdad?* Now we got that settled."

"Fellow," the marshal said grimly, "nothing's settled! What you do around here you'll do according to the rules. How long you'll stay'll depend on what I say."

Ross Varney read Lake Ellard perfectly. The marshal's only hope of survival lay in kinging it over every person in the camp. He must put every newcomer in his place — a secondary place — immediately upon arrival. Having once made a statement, there was no backing down possible. So here was a showdown forced upon him within twenty minutes of his coming into Rayo. The problem was — should he yield for the moment, thinking of the errand which had brought him up from the border or —

Partly it was his natural belligerence, and the confidence in himself born of four years of steady warfare over the Mexican line; the feeling that Ellard or any of his satellites could equal at gunplay he whom the Mexicans, crossing themselves fearfully, called *El Tecolote,* the Owl. But there was another angle to the situation.

21

A man coming as a stranger to such a place as this could not afford to take one step backward. It would mean too many steps to be taken backward. If he permitted the marshal to outface him, that would mean only that others of the marshal's faction would come up to measure themselves against him.

"Not at all!" he told the marshal grimly. "I've been in quite some few places and I stayed as long as I wanted to. Rayo's not a bit different to me. I stay here as long as I want to, minding such rules as look right to me. And there's no sense to putting off the showdown. If you think you're going to have *me* eating out of your hand — well, we might just as well step out into the street right now and settle the business!"

The silent onlookers gasped together. Since Rayo had known Lake Ellard, no man had thus flatly thrown down the glove to the marshal. Ross waited, ready to go into action with his flashing cross arm draw here, if the marshal so decided. But if Ellard's fingers quivered convulsively, they made no upward motion toward the pearl handles of his ornate guns.

"Fellow!" he barely breathed. "This is one camp where we got law and order. The marshal don't go shooting it out on the street with any pup as comes along on the prod. But here's what he does do, by God! He tells that pup to get out of camp and if the pup's got savvy, he gets. If he don't —"

"Yeh? If he don't, what does the marshal pup do?"

Interruption came, in the form of a huge and gray man who burst unceremoniously through the swinging doors of the Swan. He wore but one gun and that was jammed into the waistband of his overalls. His sun-squinted hazel eyes were flaming now. Behind him came three lean, brown young-sters with Winchesters in the crooks of their arms.

"Ellard!" the big man roared. "You're get-ting mighty close to the end of your rope! You got Terry Zeno from behind, knowing it'd bring Troop up here where you could gang him. And you did!"

"Troop asked for it," the marshal drawled, without sign of emotion. "As for you, Yocum Nowle, you better be careful you don't go the same way and for the same reason. Which is trying to ride roughshod over the authorities of Rayo. You was the curly wolf of Rayo County until the law came. Now, you're sore because you can't run things to suit yourself. Troop was the same. He tried to run the town. And it can't be done. I'm running Rayo!"

"You won't be — long!" Yocum Nowle promised him furiously. "You'll be hightailing it — if you're right lucky. And this gang of scum you're protecting — they'll be doing a cottonwood prance to Boot Hill!"

So this was Yocum Nowle — his dead father's old friend. Ross had been watching the scene with interest, and he could not see how the grim old cowman was to get out of the Swan after this declaration of war. He kept his eyes on the tense faces behind Lake Ellard — brutal faces, in the main. Now he saw what he had been expecting to see for minutes. He moved back a little toward the door, so that the man he watched could see him.

"You in the red shirt!" he called suddenly. "Keep your hands away from that gun or you'll beat that cottonwood prance!"

The slender youth in the red shirt, whose hand had been sneaking toward a black, curving butt, glared furiously at Ross. But finding too many eyes upon him, he obeyed the command, his yellow eyes coming at last to Ross's face in a snaky promise.

Yocum Nowle was staring hard at Ross, as were others — the marshal, for instance. But the big cowman was fairly gaping, as if

24

incredulous of what he saw. Ross grinned at him.

"About ready to go?" he asked. "All right! Nobody here's going to start anything."

He slid forward until he stood beside Nowle. The cowman moved backward. With Nowle's punchers covering the men inside the saloon with cocked Winchesters, the party withdrew.

"We'd better get back down-street to the sheriff's office," Nowle grunted. "I don't figure Ellard'll start a row with me right now, but you never can tell for sure, with a rattler like him."

But they reached the town's, edge — Ross leading his horse — and rounded a corner to where a two-room adobe housed jail and sheriff's office, without hostile incident.

"Go on in," invited Nowle, and Ross went inside. He heard the cowman grunt orders to the cowboys to stay outside and keep guard, as he perched himself upon the edge of the battered pine table in the center of the office.

"You're Ross Varney!" Nowle said, coming in to stand staring once more. "How come you're rambling up this way, son? I knew your pa in the old days, before he headed for the River."

"Just looking," Ross shrugged, noncommittally.

"What's become of the V Slash? Heard about your pa gettin' wiped out, but I always thought the V Slash was a real big outfit."

"It was," Ross nodded. Suddenly, from nose to chin, twin white lines showed in his brown face. "But — didn't you hear how Dad was killed? Mig' Mora came over the river, got Dad from behind a rock, killed off most of the men, and went back with every head of stock on the place. I was in Santone, at school. Quirk Ables got the range now; I sold the bare land to him for almost nothing."

"What did you do — about Mig' Mora?" Nowle's hard, hazel eyes bored into Ross's face expectantly.

"Oh, raised hell around the edges of his place for a while, until I got a chance at him."

Thus lightly did Ross dismiss the history of four years of guerilla warfare, financed by the money obtained from Quirk Ables, which had given him his nickname of "Tecolote" and had ended with the death of the killer Miguel Mora — until that day of meeting called the fastest gunman along the Rio Grande.

"If you want a job, I can put you to work,"

Nowle said, half-absently. "If your pa never slacked up in his last years, you ought to be a good hand. Good enough, anyhow."

"Who's going to be sheriff now?" Ross asked, ignoring the offer.

"Don't know. . . . Half-dozen I can think of I'd like to get. Us county commissioners'll have to appoint one for a spell, I reckon. Could hold a special election, but Ellard's gang'd likely fight like hell to put in one of their outfit. So we won't take a chance on that happening!"

He slumped into a chair and scowled at his boot toes. Ross watched him with small, unreadable smile on thin lips. Certain thoughts were revolving in Ross's mind; they roused in him a sardonic amusement.

"We got just about every damn' outlaw this side Milk River in Rayo," Yocum Nowle growled. "Things are just about on the edge of the Big Showdown. Us old-timers have got to make a stand or get pushed over the edge. Bank-robbing, cow-rustling, horse-stealing, sticking up the stage, murder and highway robbery — we've got 'em all. An' if we didn't have enough scalawags already, we're likely to get 'em. One of the boys was asleep behind the livery corral up-street yesterday, and he heard some of Ellard's gang talking about that damn' border thief,

Tecolote, heading this way. Reckon you know about him — the fellow that stuck up a big cow-trader close to Allerton and carried off the fellow's girl as they was going to get married. Heard of that?"

"Not just that way," Ross said slowly, with eyes on the hand which held his cigarette with iron steadiness. "No-o, not just like that."

"Well, that's about the facts of the business." Nowle shrugged. "Somebody sent the news to Ellard and that gang's cocked and primed for this 'Owl.' "

"Must be why they welcomed me so, today." Ross grinned absently. "Maybe they figured me as El Tecolote, in disguise."

Old Nowle chuckled deep in his chest.

"Don't reckon so, son. You look about as much like what you are as a fellow could. Nobody'd figure *you* for nothing but a plain cowboy. Have trouble with Ellard —"

"Why" — Ross smiled whimsically down at his cigarette — "he told me while I was in Rayo I'd live by the rules. His rules."

"That's the way he always meets a stranger," Yocum Nowle nodded. "You want to watch out for that yellow-eyed boy you called, today. That's Buckshot — no other name I know of. Second to Ellard — and Ellard's the fastest proposition ever *I* saw with the Colts — Buckshot is a ringtailed whizzer. And he'd just as soon kill you from behind. What did you say to Ellard?"

Ross laughed softly, amusedly. "Asked him to come out in the street and let his wolf loose," he drawled.

"My lord!" Yocum Nowle breathed, stiffening where he sat. "You — you told *Ellard* that?"

"What else could I tell him?" Ross's tone betrayed vast surprise. "He was trying to run a blazer over me. Of course, I saw him down the sheriff, but that was out of the saloon; you wouldn't say it was a real gunfight. So I didn't think about Ellard being faster than anybody in particular, with those fancy Colts of his — faster than me, for instance."

"Oh, lord!" Nowle sighed. "Son, I swear, I don't see how you got as big as you are. Only way I can figure is, you must've been a *powerful* big baby! This here Ellard, son, he'd eat you alive and then go hunting him a meal. He — Look here!"

Abruptly he got to his feet. The long-barreled, black-handled Colt he wore hung a little slantingly in the waistband of his overalls. He fished in a pocket and brought out a silver dollar. With his left hand, he flipped the coin upward toward the ceiling.

Before it struck the floor, his right hand had darted to the Colt's butt, the long weapon leaped out to cover Ross. Nowle nodded sardonically to the respectfully intent younger man.

"Ellard, son, is even faster'n *that!*"

"I see," Ross said, nothing but courteous impressment showing in his brown face. "I like that stunt. Let's see what *I* could do with it. . . ."

He drew alternately the right and left hand guns from his holsters and ejected five shells from each, then replaced the Colts and glanced down at their hang. From his pants pocket came a handful of coins. He selected a silver quarter. This he placed on the wrist of his right hand and extended that hand, then his left, until his arms were horizontal, at right and left angles to his body.

Suddenly he turned his right wrist, letting the coin go. Down streaked his hands. Out of the holsters leaped the twin Colts, Ross's thumbs snapping back the big hammers. Four times he clicked each Colt before the quarter rang upon the wooden floor of the sheriff's office. Nowle sagged in the big chair, mouth slightly open beneath his ropy gray mustache. Ross grinned at him faintly, then stooped to recover his shells.

"Another — accident, Mr. Cowboy from

the River?" a cool voice inquired from the doorway behind them both.

CHAPTER THREE

Yocum Nowle turned his head to stare dully at his niece. The motion seemed mechanical. Ross was watching her steadily and in his dark blue eyes was somber reflection of certain unpleasant thoughts.

"I've been outside the door, listening and watching, for several minutes," the girl told her uncle. "When you got ready to show this — deceptive young man the quick draw, I almost interfered. For I have seen you practice the draw and, this morning, I saw Mr. Varney draw at the gallop and smash a rattler's head. Then I thought that you had better see, than hear, in this instance."

"You hadn't ought to come to town, Marie," Nowle growled. "Ed —"

"I haven't seen Ed," she shrugged. "And when Hector Olsen rode out with word of Sheriff Troop's killing and I recalled that you were in town, I brought in Withers and Hendy, to back whatever rash move you might make when you heard of Troop's death. It happened that we were in the north pasture when Hector came by, so we got here quickly."

"You could've sent them two in without coming yourself," Nowle grumbled. "But it's all right, now. I got to get busy. We got to have a sheriff — a salty one! And we got to have him *yesterday!* There's some good old-timers we can get."

"Ellard would make doll rags out of those good old-timers!" Marie said scornfully. "In their day they were curly wolves, but now they're just as Troop was — too old; slow; over-cautious. Why think about *importing* a sheriff, anyway? Hasn't Fate sent you as good material as you could ask? If there's a man between Milk River and the Rio Grande who has a chance against Ellard, it's — Ross Varney, here!"

"By Joe!" Nowle grunted. "Funny I never thought of that! But — you're sort of young, Ross."

Ross moved his wide shoulders a thought impatiently. This being discussed as a horse who might or might not serve to win a race he found irritating to his pride.

"Seems to me," he said coldly, "that you take a good deal for granted! Who told you *I* was a candidate for your blame' job, anyhow? It's just possible, you know, that I've got business of my own to attend to — business that's bigger in my eye than your troubles here!"

The girl was standing before him in two swift steps, almost before he had finished. She held out both small hands appealingly and the brown eyes were widened, pleading.

"Please don't take our talk that way! We're at our wits' ends, really. We *have* to do something to make Rayo County a safe place to live once more. Since half the officers — the town-half — are in league with the criminals, the sheriff has the hardest task a sheriff ever had in this country. It isn't mere gunplay he faces. That would be a comparatively simple problem. He has to cope with crooked legal processes, too; the law that can be invoked by Ellard's faction. I ask you to take Troop's star. Won't you do it — *please!* — Ross Varney?"

Ross stared uncertainly at his feet. He had an idea that something more than the reason she voiced was responsible for this plea. And women were pretty much alike, regardless of their class. If you stopped to think about it, a pretty dance-hall girl, trying to persuade a cowboy to buy more drinks, tried all the little tricks of persuasion that this girl was using, now. She was working on his sympathy; working on his vanity . . .

"It was bad enough with only Ellard and

33

his gang," Marie said suddenly. "But now we're going to have that awful bandit from the border. El Tecolote, you know. Perhaps Uncle Yocum told you?"

"Do you want me to take the job?" Ross snapped viciously at Nowle. He was moved by a purely sardonic impulse to put the question. He would take their damn' job; he would shove Ellard and his gang over the edge; then he would say to these Nowles, uncle and niece, "The Owl bids you goodby!"

"Sure do," Yocum Nowle nodded. "You fooled me proper at first and I'm ready to admit it. And I'm free to tell you I think you've got the best chance of anybody I know to clean up Rayo County — and be with us when we celebrate the cleaning."

"Dying's just about the last thing I figure to do," Ross nodded dryly. "If I didn't think that there was an even chance to be with you all, on that day you're talking about, I probably wouldn't take the job with you. Now — I want to know some things!

"Who's Ellard? Where did he come from? Who's backing him? What are the formalities when I make an arrest? Who's district judge? What kind of onion is he? Who's got possession of your county machinery and how about grand juries? Lawyers?"

"Good lord!" Nowle gasped "You never studied law none, yourself, did you? I swear you sound like a lawyer."

"Let me tell him, Uncle Yocum," the girl said quickly. "He's quite right. He mustn't move blindly — *here*."

Ross eyed her somewhat narrowly. He was not wholly accustomed to extremely lovely young ladies who knew every feminine trick and wile and yet could turn so businesslike in a flash. But there was unwilling admiration in his eyes as she turned to him swiftly, seeming to take Nowle's consent for granted.

"Ellard's an old-time faro dealer and gunman. He's been everywhere — all over the frontier. He drifted to Rayo with other gunmen, many of them old friends of his. Men like Uncle Yocum here — there are quite a few in the country — hardly understood what was taking place until there was an election and Lake Ellard was made City Marshal."

She shrugged.

"There had been crime here, before. There had been killings over claims jumped and horses and cattle stolen. But since Ellard's election we've had a man for breakfast very frequently. And as for miscellaneous and assorted crimes — well, the Junction stage carrying passengers, express and bullion has been robbed so often that the driver says the horses pull up instinctively whenever a man steps into the road!

"These outlaws are all protected by Ellard. Buckshot and Rod Backers, to mention only two of the outstanding ones, boast openly of their robberies and murders. Buckshot gives dance-hall girls here the jewelry taken that day from stage passengers. You ask about judges, lawyers, grand juries —

"Ellard is backed by what is called a 'Law and Order' faction. There's too much else occupying the lawful element's time to permit it watching very closely the methods of its officers, The big mining men and merchants and bankers are too busy making money while the camp booms to interfere. And, within the town's limits, Ellard does keep order. In this way — most of the killings can be called 'legal' because they're done by Ellard and his deputies. That yellow-eyed Buckshot is one; Rod Backers another.

"The grand jury is in continuous session. That means that if you're 'short' in Rayo, you'll find that the District Attorney has managed to get your name on a warrant. God help you if you're caught where Ellard and his gang can try to serve it on you. The coroner's jury will report that you were killed while resisting arrest. The district judge — Xavier — is all right. But he doesn't know what he is doing half the time. He'd have to be a mind-reader, actually to know!"

"Madre de dios!" Ross gasped, shaking his head dizzily. "And you think El Tecolote could worry *this* country! Why, these buzzards'd make him look like an amateur! Tell me! Who killed this deputy sheriff? The one whose killing sent Troop up to get his?"

"Rod Backers," Nowle said. "I didn't see him in the Swan today. But there's a bunch of witnesses to the murder. And it was done practically from behind. Terry Zeno played a damn' fool, going into the Swan at all. But he was minding his own business until Buckshot shot him from off to one side. Troop was trying to arrest Backers when he was killed."

"What kind of gentleman is this Backers? Besides being a gunman — which, of course, he has to be."

"Long-coupled jigger. Wears his hair down to his shoulder and has buckskin fringe on his sleeves and pants-legs. Black eyes and hair. Two guns and anyhow one bowie down the back of his neck. He'd rather get his man from behind than from the front, but he will shoot it out if he's crowded."

A corner of Ross's hard mouth lifted whimsically — ruefully almost. The girl, watching him with tense brown eyes, frowned a little and leaned forward where she sat. "You — you don't mean to try to arrest Backers? Not after — after what happened to Troop?"

Ross's face hardened quickly.

"There's one thing I meant to tell you before I promised to take the job: If I'm the sheriff, then I'm certainly going to be the whole blame' sheriff's office! The only thing I'll be held responsible for is results — and for them only after a reasonable time. I don't want a bunch of county commissioners rawhiding me because I didn't — or did — do something or other. As a matter of fact, I won't stand for that!"

Yocum Nowle's weathered face turned beet red at this flat pronunciamento. But if he intended angry retort to this bold youngster, the sound of feet at the door checked him.

"Sure, I'm telling you I want to see someone inside," came a full-toned bellow. "She's the sheriff's office, is she not? She's public property, is she not? Well, then! Sure I've as good a right as any to go inside."

Nowle scowled, but Ross moved gently toward the doorway and stood, smiling a little, staring out. And with his appearance, magically the argument ceased.

"Let that fellow in, will you, boys?" Ross said to the watching riflemen.

He stood back and inside came a squat, long-armed man of about his own age, carrying a .44 Winchester carbine in the crook of his arm. This newcomer stopped short and his small blue eyes roved curiously from Nowle to the girl. His was a pugnacious face, square-chinned, gash-mouthed, with long, Irish upper lip.

"I'm the sheriff of Rayo County," Ross said softly. "Something for you?"

"The sheriff?" repeated the other, looking fixedly at Ross. "Huh! Myself, I'm Pat Phelan. I hail from the World-at-Large. How's for a job at deputying?"

"Any — qualifications?" Ross asked, fingers busied with cigarette-building, watching Yocum Nowle's scowl from the corner of an amused blue eye.

"I don't know what qualifications you'd ask of your deputy," Pat Phelan replied thoughtfully. "But whatever they may be, you may rest assured I've got 'em. I was a deputy city marshal at Fort Worth onct — for three weeks."

"Why did you quit?" asked Yocum Nowle.

"Why, in a town the like of Fort Worth, the marshal must be the hardest of the hard. Particularly, he must be the hardest on the force — and with me decorating a star, you understand that he could never be!"

"I'm going down to the Swan Saloon to make an arrest," Ross said. "And there's a gang down there, headed by the city marshal, which'll likely object. In fact, it's a real showdown, this arrest."

"Why don't we be starting then?" Pat inquired, casting a hungry glance at the lever-action riot gun hanging on the office wall.

Chapter Four

Ross threw back his head and laughed outright. Yocum Nowle grinned, too, if unwillingly, one might have thought. Only the girl watched with pale face and widened eyes.

"Want to wait here till we get back?" Ross asked Nowle. "No, no! Don't want you along. Either we go by ourselves or we have to take a young army. Wait here and see how things come out."

And with a double-nod — to Pat Phelan and at the riot gun — he moved toward the door. The girl came to her feet, lips parting as if to protest. But Ross was outside and the squat Phelan, moving with speed hardly to be expected in his bulk, had snatched the shotgun, snapped the lever to see that it was loaded, then slid out after Ross.

They went back up the street toward the Swan, Ross whistling softly to himself. Phelan hastened alongside. "How come?" he inquired simply. "The sheriff, the girl, and all?"

"How come you trailed me?" Ross countered. "Thought you were to stay at Alamito and wait for me?"

"Sure and you'll have to blame my corns," Pat Phelan meditated aloud. "The third one on my left foot took to hurting and to myself I says, 'Sure and Ross's damn' recklessness has got him into something! Pat, my son, it's better you throw a hull onto Shamrock and be on your way. Without your careful nature to be controlling him, Pat,' I says to myself, 'why, sure there's no telling what that omadhaun'll be up to.' "

"Oh, lord!" Ross groaned. "Where are the others?"

"At Alamito. Sure, I promised the last of them full sets of store teeth if they moved before they'd word from us. Who's it we'll be gathering in?"

"Long-haired gunman named Backers. Don't know just how I'm going to do this trick, Pat, but you slide along the wall, here, to that window. Looks like it's open. Be ready to show yourself in it if I need you. I'm going on inside."

At this twilight hour, Rayo was very much alive. Free in the town were a couple hundred of miners off shift, seeking entertainment in saloon and dance-place and gambling hell. Lone wolves were there too — roughly clad prospectors in for a fresh supply of grub or a spree. The cowboys from outlying ranches were apt to favor the little town of Rawles, twelve miles to the northwest, where "everything went," but there was a liberal sprinkling of the wide-hatted, booted fraternity in Rayo — keeping somewhat close together. It was quite alive, Rayo. Quite!

Ross, moving into the shadows of the wooden awning before the Swan, made the door without seeming to attract any attention from those on the rude veranda. In the doorway he stopped for a swift glance across the swinging doors. No sign of Lake Ellard — none of Rod Backers or the young Buckshot, at first glance. From the stares he collected, he surmised that there were some here now who had witnessed his argument with Ellard in the afternoon.

But he came with placid face to the bar and ordered a drink. And in that minute he saw well down the long bar a lanky, dark-eyed man who could hardly be other than Rod Backers, killer of the deputy sheriff. Backers was looking straight at him. Still no trace of either Ellard or Buckshot — he of the malevolent yellow eyes. And something overheard — a casual conversation on Ross's right — as he stood facing the bar, might explain Buckshot's absence, if not the marshal's.

"— and he had nerve enough to say right in Buckshot's face that *he* wasn't worryin' about nobody liftin' his roll. An' when he went out to find when the stage left, Buckshot, he looks at me an' he grins. Then he hitches up his belts an' goes driftin' too. . . ."

It was two habitués gossiping over their drinks, and certainly it seemed typical of that Rayo which Marie had described to Ross, that they discussed the probabilities of robbery and murder by the deputy city marshal so openly. But if Buckshot were absent on "business," that still did not explain Ellard's absence. There was a nice point of etiquette here: If Ross tried to make an arrest in the town itself, without word to the marshal, then forever after he must ignore Ellard. But if he went to Ellard and announced his intention of taking Backers in —

But Rod Backers, perhaps conceiving that he had a position to maintain as the only evident peace officer of Rayo, solved a part of Ross's problem. He came elbowing his way through the crowd of men along the bar, until he had shouldered in beside Ross. He was of about Ross's height, so violet-blue eyes and murky black met in a level, searching scrutiny. Backers had both thumbs hooked in crossed cartridge-belts; his hands were not four inches above his gunbutts.

"Who are you?" he demanded truculently, scowling.

"The High Sheriff of Rayo County!" Ross informed him evenly. "You're Rod Backers, deputy marshal? Like to have a little wawa with you, off to one side."

Into the small black eyes leaped a gleam of animal-like alertness. The long dirty-nailed hands hooked in cartridge-belts tightened convulsively. Ross let his own gaze wander toward Backers's hands, then return a shade contemptuously to the killer's tight face.

"Anything you got to say to me you can say right here!"

"What I've got to say could be said here, all right," Ross nodded. "But that don't mean it ought to be said here, or that it'd be better said here. Of course, if you feel nervous about talking to me — not to say downright scared to get out of this bar-room — Hell! There's just one of me, you know. And if one man can't take you off to the side and say something to you. . . ."

On the edge of the listening mass someone laughed. Rod Backers did not turn his head to find the source of the laughter, but his lean face went red, while suspiciously his black eyes bored into Ross's.

"Come on out!" he snarled. "Any time Rod Backers is worried about three the likes of you —"

Ross led the way to the swinging doors, but before pushing them open, stopped short. He turned to face Backers, two steps behind him.

"Will that gang in there get so interested in our talk that they'll come sticking their noses over our shoulders? Or have you got 'em educated enough to mind their own business?"

"You all stay in here!" Backers commanded the restless crowd in the bar-room, but with a shade of unwillingness in his voice, as if Ross were forcing him to the action. "Me and this fellow'll do whatever talking's to be done and I won't need no horning in from nobody!"

Ross went on out and turned left, wondering how far Backers would trail before balking. He had reached the edge of a store veranda when the lank deputy marshal checked him with a snarling hail, "How far you think you got to go?"

Ross waited until Backers caught up with him, then, "You're supposed to be hell on wheels with your guns, Backers," he breathed. "Well, I'm going to put a proposition to you, fair and square. I want you to come along with me to jail, charged with the murder of Terry Zeno. It'll be a plumb legal arrest; you'll have a chance to make bond and stand trial and all. But if you don't submit peacefully to arrest — well, we'll just have to have our showdown here and now; I don't *think* you'd have a Chinaman's chance to outshoot me, but I'll give you an even break!"

In the dim light from a neighboring oil-lamp, he could see Backers, utterly taken aback, crouched like a waiting jaguar with hands clenched into ready claws just over the butts of his low-swung Colts. Ross waited, smiling tight-lipped.

"Go to hell!" Backers snarled and there

was the slap, audible for yards, of his palms on gunbutts.

Ross went into action with hands that moved like striking snake-heads. Before Backers's muzzles had cleared holster-tops, Ross shot him twice and was stooped over the crumpled figure, wresting the guns from nerveless hands. A squat shadow glided from beneath a wooden awning and Pat Phelan was covering with deadly riot gun the street in the direction from which they had come.

"Watch 'em, Pat!" Ross snapped. "Cover my back while I pack this beef!"

And he swung Backers up diagonally across his back, so that the deputy marshal's head hung over his shoulder. And then he whirled and went swiftly, as if the burden were nothing, toward the sheriff's office. From the Swan's direction came a muffled, wordless roar — the mob voice. Ross's eyes shone like sunlit steel as he listened. Then came thought of Marie in the office and he swore viciously. The girl would have to be got out of there.

"Back, you hellions!" he heard Pat Phelan bellow. "Faith, the High Sheriff of Rayo County is making an arrest and we're needing no help from the likes of you all! Back with you, else I'll be showing you the insides of this riot gun!"

Figures came running to meet Ross. He still had a Colt in his right hand, for he gripped Rod Backers's wrist with his left. He snapped up the weapon's muzzle, then lowered it, making out Yocum Nowle's bulk in the dimness.

"Ross!" Nowle called tensely. "You all right?"

"Finer than frog-hair!" Ross chuckled. "Help Phelan discourage that gang, will you? I'm going to slam Backers in the coop."

He broke into a trot and so entered the office. Marie stood aside to let him pass to the barred door of the jail behind. Unbelievingly, it seemed, she stared. Mingled with admiration in her face was another emotion — a sort of puzzlement; wonderment; worry. Louder, now, from outside, came the roar of the mob. She paled. Ross reappeared from the jail cell. He grinned at her.

"Get in there, will you, and tie him up. He's not dead; I got him through the shoulders. *Hike!*"

Then he leaped to the door, where Nowle and his three Winchester-bearing cowboys stood with Pat. Up the street moved steadily the dark mass from town. Ross was beside Pat, taking the riot gun from him, before the watchers noted him.

"Only place they can break in is right here, at the front," Ross said. "Now, here, all of you skip inside to the windows — and shut and lock the front door! In with you, Pat, blame' your soul. Don't stand there arguing with me, you bull-headed Irish terrier! I'm Sheriff of Rayo County and, *por dios!* I'm going to prove it to that mob. If I can't hold my own jail against all comers, I'm better off dead!"

Reluctantly, they obeyed him. He heard the clang of the iron-sheathed door, followed by the thuds of heavy bars falling. And with wide-brimmed hat thrust back upon tousled yellow hair, with violet-blue eyes turned slaty hard, dull shining, he lifted the riot gun and held it with two hands.

"Halt!" he hailed the oncoming mass. Then, with queer sardonic lift of the mouth corners as the words came to mind, "In the name of the Law! Halt where you are! It's Sheriff Varney talking!"

They stopped, but as that sinister muzzle moved back and forth, covering their front, from two hundred throats came the spine-crinkling rumble. Ross grinned and continued to move the riot gun's muzzle. "Then, if you don't want to halt," he said in conversational tone, "come on!"

And he added the fighting word of the old West. . . .

CHAPTER FIVE

For an instant that mob surged forward. Ross found time to wonder, even as he speculated concerning his chances of stopping the advance, if this dark mass of men here did not represent virtually the whole of Marshal Ellard's faction in Rayo. At any rate, he thought, with mouth lifting slightly at a corner, it was nothing if not a salty crew!

"Come on!" he called to them again, speaking levelly. "There's enough in your gang — even of your kind — to handle one man. But — I'll certainly gather me the first man that makes a move to shoot. You can take that as you like. You don't have to believe me."

The front rank stopped. What Ross told them was all too true. He was a dead man if any chose to flip back a Colt-hammer — but two, or three, or four in that front rank would surely be as dead. Those behind pushed upon those in front. But the men directly before those muzzles dug in their heels and upon their faces showed the beginning of a change in emotions — the breaking up of their savage determination to rescue their lieutenant from the jail, and settle this unpleasant personage with the shotgun; some thought of the gaping wounds left by buckshot. . . .

"*Git!*" Ross said suddenly, sensing the precisely correct moment. "*Git!*"

Up a little he lifted the twin muzzles of his riot gun. His face gleamed paper white in the dusk; his eyes shone with a sort of impersonal savagery. A man in the front rank, on one end, slipped aside into the shadows. Another followed. And in this instant there sounded the thudding of hoofs — hoofs of galloping horses — from behind the building Ross Varney guarded.

Around the corner of the jail surged a solid mass of riders, looming gigantic, sinister, in the dimness of the evening lights. The marshal's following simply melted at this apparent reinforcement of the sheriff. Ross watched them go, then turned slowly to stare at these riders. A figure slipped gracefully from the saddle; Ross found himself facing a man as tall as himself. This one leaned slightly forward to stare into Ross's face.

"Who are you?" inquired the newcomer. "I was looking for Yocum Nowle."

"I'm Varney, the new sheriff. Nowle's inside."

"Well, let's go in, then. Your friends —

and mine — have hightailed it."

"Open up, Pat!" Ross called, wondering who this man might be.

The heavy door swung open and the tall man moved that way without waiting on Ross, who followed thoughtfully.

Inside, Nowle, the cowboys and Pat Phelan stood with rifles in the crooks of their arms; the cowboys were grinning a trifle relievedly; Nowle's heavy face was set like a rock; Pat Phelan looked thoughtfully up from beneath brick-colored brows and whistled softly.

Marie Nowle came to the door of the jail and stood staring into the sheriff's office. Ross watched her for an instant. She was looking at the tall man with a sort of rigidity observable in expression and posture both.

"Hello, Nowle!" the tall man said easily. "And Miss Nowle! This is a real pleasure!"

" 'Lo, Kawrie," the cowman nodded without cordiality. The girl merely inclined her head slightly.

Ross came on in and moved so that he faced the man called Kawrie. There was a dare-devil something even in the set of Kawrie's back, which Ross found highly interesting. This devil-may-care attitude was mirrored in the dark, handsome face, with its high cheekbones and thin-lipped mouth; mirrored most strongly in the large, full-lidded black eyes.

"We heard, over in Rawles, that Troop had been downed," Kawrie smiled. "So Vic Lundy and I gathered a few of the boys together and we came over to mingle a bit with Rayo's beloved marshal. Troop was more of a good buggy horse than a fighting stallion, but we've sort of backed his play all along and Ellard's killing of him was just a little too pointed. Heard the uproar down here, so we drove up and hitched."

"If you had arrived five minutes earlier, I'd have been downright grateful to you," Ross drawled.

Kawrie turned clear around and looked Ross over with the impersonal interest a man displays in a horse. From head to foot he studied Ross, who watched him, in his turn, with a little humorless lip-widening that could have passed for a smile — and with the dawning of understanding.

"And why," Kawrie said slowly, "don't you feel gratitude as it is?"

"The mob had just thought of something up-street," Ross explained. "They were going to attend to it. . . ."

"My dear man, if we hadn't ridden up when we did" — Kawrie's tone was tolerant

53

to an extreme — "that outfit would have made a meal of you!"

"Could have," Ross corrected him with widening of his thin smile. "But — with a ten-gauge riot gun, I'd have got me a light lunch. . . ."

Kawrie was regarding him more steadily than before, when a slim youngster in early twenties came swaggering through the door. He was at this moment somewhat swollen around his gray eyes; more than a trifle puffy in his boyishly good-looking face. And his clothing, an expensive, almost dudish cowboy outfit, looked as if it had been very recently slept in.

Seeing everything without seeming to focus upon anything in particular, Ross observed the increased grimness of Yocum Nowle's expression at sight of this youth; noted Marie Nowle's quick, appealing glance in the boy's direction. But as he came in, hitching up the crossed cartridge-belts that held up his long-barreled Colts, the cowboy seemed to heed neither niece or uncle.

"Where you been, Ed?" Nowle demanded.

"Around," the boy shrugged sulkily. "Come in with Keith, here, to mix into whatever was going to happen."

"Thought you was supposed to be helping

wrestle them three-year-olds on Blue Creek . . . ?"

It was not hard to guess the check Nowle was keeping on his speech, as he faced the sulky young figure.

"I was — and I ain't!" Ed growled defiantly. "What are you running, anyhow, a penitentiary? There's enough men over there to handle twice the stuff they're working. So I — rode around a little."

Yocum Nowle eyed him with grim intentness. Keith Kawrie watched the pair with a half-mocking, half-malicious smile on his thin mouth. It was as if he awaited a climactic something here — a situation he knew was inevitable.

"Ed," Nowle said slowly, "I swear I don't know what to do about you. I give you every chance a man could give his boy and you just won't work. You can't be depended on to do anything — except to do what you oughtn't to do. You're taking my money every payday and giving me nothing in the way of work. You —"

"All right, then, take your damn' job and give it to somebody that suits you!" Ed snarled. "I'm through!"

He whirled and went out, the slight unsteadiness of his walk explaining in part the rumpled condition of his clothing. Yocum

Nowle stared after him without change of face. But Marie was pale. Kawrie's malicious grin deepened and Nowle seemed to feel the tall man's amusement. He turned and looked at Kawrie with a calculating narrowness of hazel eyes. Kawrie grinned the more.

"Stage was robbed again this afternoon," he remarked, conversationally.

Ross, conscious of cross-currents here which he did not understand, was watching everyone. Now, it seemed to him, Nowle's face set a little harder, as if the lazy voice had carried to him a message in code — a message he had dreaded. Evidently, it bore meaning to the girl, too. She stared with horror-stricken eyes at Keith Kawrie.

"That" — Ross entered the conversation with a drawl as lazy as Kawrie's own — "is something we're going to call a halt on."

"If it isn't our sheriff again!" Kawrie cried, turning once more upon Ross. "With a promise!"

"With a promise!" Ross nodded, smilingly. "I notice that there's a lot of politics in Rayo County. Sort of criss-cross. I'm guessing that the county's got rather more thieves than one county's got any use for; so many that they've split up into sides and parties."

"The oracle speaks!" Kawrie nodded, with

56

mock admiration. "Go on, young sir!"

"I am! Being a newcomer, it's hard for me to understand all the ins and outs of things — so I won't try! Only way I can work is to be one of those fellows without fear or favor you hear so much about before elections. I'm going to have to hang the deadwood on the outlaws regardless of where they vote and pull 'em in high, wide and handsome."

"Mr. Sheriff!" Kawrie cried, grinning widely, "you're a man after my own heart! You, come to us as a sentient image of Justice, bearing a torch in one hand, a six-gun in the other, so to speak. I want to assure you that in your new duties, which you have so auspiciously entered upon today, you have my whole-hearted sympathy and good wishes. I assure you, also, that in your efforts to rid Rayo County of its malefactors, I will assist in every way possible — so far as my interests permit. . . . Won't I — won't we, Vic?"

"Sure will!" a harsh voice answered from the doorway, very heartily.

Ross turned slightly sideway, to inspect the last speaker. He saw a squat, hard-faced, yet seemingly good-humored man slouching in the door with a heavy shoulder against the jamb, thumbs hooked in the waistband of his overalls, little black eyes

57

twinkling as he listened to Kawrie.

"Thanks," Ross nodded, grinning at Kawrie, in his turn. "I'll surely use you — all I can. About this stage robbery today — how much do you know about it?"

"My dear man," Kawrie cried, in pained accents, "how could I know anything about it, save that it occurred? Doubtless, it was engineered by men of Ellard's faction. We — Vic and I and our friends — hold as much aloof from the lawlessness so prevalent in Rayo County as — well, as circumstances permit."

"I'll bet you do!" Ross nodded gravely. "Well, I'll just have to look into this."

"Meanwhile," Kawrie said, "my friends and I must be getting back to Rawles. Come over, Mr. Sheriff, and see us soon. It's just a small place, but our citizens are certainly up and doing. I promise you'll be thoroughly entertained."

"I don't doubt that a bit," Ross nodded. "I'll surely be over to have a look at you, soon's the time's right. . . ."

"Good night, Nowle!" Kawrie said.

Then he moved past the big, silent cowman and took both of Marie's hands in his.

Ross thought the girl let him hold her hands half-unwillingly, but only half. Certainly, he thought grimly, this devil-may-care figure, obviously a renegade from some good family, was a man to take the average woman's eye. She might look askance at his doings, but a dare-devil manner, polished speech, go far with women, Ross decided gloomily.

"Good night, Miss Nowle," Kawrie said in that actor's voice of his, that could alter and shift like the tone of running water. "I hope to see you again — soon. And I —"

He bent nearer her and whispered something — something which evidently did not displease her. Then, with quick, smiling nod to those in the office, he went out. And certainly, as Ross had decided, he was a splendid figure of a man. Ross, who had missed not the slightest move of either Kawrie or the girl, watched him go with the thought that when the shooting began in Rayo County, it would suit him very well to face Keith Kawrie at the very first.

CHAPTER SIX

Ross stood listening to the riders outside until they whirled their horses and the thudding of hoofs grew fainter. After a couple of minutes, there rose above the dulling pound a high, shrill yell in which many voices blended, accompanied by the rolling of six-shooters. Pat Phelan grinned at Ross.

"Sure, he's taking 'em back up the main street, and taking 'em shooting — the nervy devil."

Ross nodded absently. He had a great deal to consider, just then. It was all very well to say blandly that he intended to arrest every criminal charged with commission of a crime, regardless of his political affiliations. It was exactly what he intended to do. But how make a start, right now? And, even if a sheriff filled his jail, would that mean conviction of his prisoners?

"What this county needs," he said suddenly, aloud, "is a good bunch of vigilantes and several coils of new, strong rope . . . *por dios!*"

He stared suddenly at Pat Phelan, blue eyes shining. Pat stared back with some bewilderment, but before Ross could speak, Yocum Nowle interrupted. "You're right about that! You can round up all the scalawags and then watch the courts turn 'em loose."

"Gents!" called someone outside the door. "There's three of us here an' we want to come in an' argue with you all. We're plumb peaceful. All right?"

"Come in — peaceful," Ross replied.

Three hard-looking citizens entered with

hands conspicuously clear of the weapons all wore. One carried a large, folded paper. This one smiled genially at Ross.

"More ways of killin' a cat than stuffin' her with axle-grease!" he remarked cryptically. "Judge Xavier is lettin' Rod Backers out on bail. District Attorney's willin'."

He extended a paper. Ross took it, opened the folds and read the order. He looked whimsically at Nowle. The three men of Ellard's faction grinned pleasantly. "All right!" Ross nodded suddenly. "You can have him."

After all, he had achieved his point in the mere arresting of Backers. He had proved that he could and would arrest one of Ellard's henchmen and that he was capable of keeping his prisoner against illegal attempts at rescue. So, as long as Ellard could do nothing to counteract the effect of the sheriff's action, the crew in Rayo would recall it. And to refuse to surrender Backers when Judge Xavier had granted him bond, would be to handicap himself seriously in talking things over with the judge — as Ross intended to do without delay.

So he nodded the three men into the jail, where Backers, bandaged by Marie Nowle, now lay upon a cot. The men helped their ally to his feet and so they went staggering in a close knot to the door. There the fellow who had delivered the bond turned for an instant to look thoughtfully at Ross.

"It won't be so much trouble, next time. . . ." he drawled.

"You figure to import a lot more gunmen?" Ross countered, and grinned. "Or is Ellard going to get a law passed against the sheriff packing a gun? Roll your hoop, fellow; roll your hoop! Tell Ellard, for me, that maybe it *won't* be so much trouble next time. Fact is, it's likely to be a lot more!"

Then he turned back to Yocum Nowle; to the silent cowboys who had taken no part in any of this discussion; to Pat Phelan, who was regarding his leader with queer, half-rueful expression.

"You might call our first butting scrape a sort of draw, I reckon," Ross grinned. "Well, Nowle?"

"Nothing," shrugged the big cowman. "I — I reckon I'll be riding back to the ranch. Marie, you want to stay with Mis' Upson, or go back with me an' the boys?"

"I'll stay here and ride home tomorrow — probably," the girl said slowly.

To Ross, who was finding much of mystery in her attitude of all the evening, it seemed that she had good reason for wishing to remain in Rayo. And he had a double-barreled puzzle to solve. With sight of Kawrie's greeting of her and her reception of his slight advances, Ross had thought the girl more than a trifle impressed by the tall leader of hardcase riders. But Ed Nowle's entry had made him wonder. Was she pulled between liking for two men?

But chiefly, at this moment, he wanted to be rid of his visitors. There was much to talk over with Pat Phelan; a very definite step to be taken. He waited courteously for them to go.

"So long, Ross," Nowle said, with Marie's reply. "See you some more — if you don't go the way Troop went. By Jiminy! You sure did more tonight than Troop ever did in his whole time — to rile up that bunch of sidewinders in town. Well, you can call yourself Sheriff. I'll see the other commissioners and we'll back you in what you see fit to do."

With a grunt to his riders and to Marie, he turned to the door. The girl seemed to dawdle to let the men go. She and Ross faced each other, then, for an instant, both heedless of Pat Phelan.

"I —" she began, then stopped short, with a quick wave of color staining her paled face. "Will you — watch for Ed? Please! He's a wild boy, but really fine under that sulky shell. And right now, he's apt to be wilder than ever."

"How about Kawrie?" Ross drawled, in tone as low as hers had been. "Shepherd him, too?"

Deeper still her cheeks were dyed at the sarcasm. Her small, firm chin jerked up.

"You'll find, Mr. Cowboy-on-the-Prod, that Keith Kawrie has a way of taking care of himself!"

And out she ran to her uncle. Ross shook his head a little, as if to clear it, then turned to Pat.

"Fast enough for you, old-timer? I sort of got stampeded into this business but, now that I'm in it, I'm certainly sticking till the last dog's hung! And there's apt to be action a-plenty before we finish sweeping up and heave away the broom."

"Vigilantes, you said," Pat drawled, reflectively, but with the dawning of a war-light in small blue eyes. "Vigilantes and a bale of rope. . . ."

"That's what I said, but I've got another thought. How many of the boys'll be at Alamito, you reckon?"

"Eleven-twelve," Pat shrugged. "Crickashaw, he may well've got thirsty by now, but sure, there'll be plenty to do this job. Want 'em?"

Ross nodded, watching amusedly. Not only in aggressive warfare of fists or Colts or Winchesters was Pat a first lieutenant above price. Their time together, bucking a leader so daring and capable as Miguel Mora, had given them the faculty of working together like right and left hands. Pat could anticipate Ross's intent; could formulate the manner of its execution; all this without words, almost.

"There's a Mexican *rancho* beyond the town, here," Pat said. "I stopped there today and talked a bit. The boy there will be glad to ride south with the word. I'll be slipping out, come morning, to start him off."

"Good enough! They're expecting El Tecolote to come riding this way. *Por dios!* They'll get more than they bargained for. Wonder who passed that word along about my riding north?"

"Sure, we've enemies enough down there, even with Mig' Mora dead where you left him," Pat shrugged. "You've found no sign of the man Sayer?"

"The young lady tells me that no such man is known around here. She seems to have a grasp of politics here, too. But I said, down south, when we got the word of old Baldy Fay's murder, that I'd settle his murderer's hash and I'm sticking to that. We'll find Matt Sayer, all right. Now let's hit the bunk. Something tells me we won't

65

do a lot of yawning on this job!"

CHAPTER SEVEN

Pat Phelan sprawled comfortably upon his cot. Going to bed involved no more than jerking off his boots, for Pat. Now, flat upon his back, he crossed his legs and alternately stared at the lifted toes of his right foot, and Ross Varney, who sat across from him. The lantern's light showed Ross as a grave young man. Pat spoke around a cigarette stub in his mouth.

"I was just thinking," he said — in a faraway voice.

Ross regarded him with cold suspicion.

"Seems to me," he remarked acidly, "that you've done that, a time or two before. And usually something comes of it — something pretty bad, if not a lot worse."

Pat drew in smoke and blew a succession of rings toward the lantern.

"Ah, now," he reproved his commander. "You're put out a bit tonight — and likely it's because of just the thing I'm thinking about now. . . ."

Ross stripped the flannel shirt from his scarred shoulders. He regarded with no lessening of suspicious expression the bland

66

smile which Pat now turned upon flexing toes.

"I was thinking about the man Kawrie," Pat drawled. "A pretty salty sort of hairpin. Not?"

Ross sat down upon his cot and began to work at a boot. In a muffled tone he said cautiously that Kawrie did seem to know his way around.

"But there are some others," he added.

"Like you and me," Pat agreed placidly. "Funny, the likes of us wearing stars."

"What's funny about it?" Ross grunted. "The man that wears the star in any town or county has to be the man who believes in the law and is willing to get his head knocked off — or shot off — keeping that law going. If you mean that we've been considered outside the law for a long while, and now discover ourselves ramming the law down the necks of men who, on the face of it, seem to be the sort we were considered — Yes, that could seem a little funny. But —"

He made a long arm and got tobacco and papers from his shirt, hanging on a chair. He shook flakes of tobacco into a paper and leveled it with a forefinger. Then, with the half-finished cigarette in thumb and finger he looked frowningly, almost blankly, at his friend.

"The point is, there are outlaws and outlaws. Some of 'em — like you and me and the boys — are the kind who haven't any real business *being* on the left side of the law. I talked to an old judge one time, about that very thing. He was one of the few lawyers I ever met that I could like. He was educated in the history of the law and he made it clear how law began back in the days when the first men came out of their caves and started a row about whose bone that was, lying under the tree. One thing he said, I've always remembered:

" 'No law is worth a damn unless it represents the opinion of the people who are going to live by that law. And, when the laws those people make are not enforced by the people they choose to carry 'em out, then the people have the right to take away from their officers the job of enforcing laws and do it themselves.' "

Pat stared at him with a small frown. "Driving your horses into *which* corral?" he demanded. "Proving what sad, serious and solitary idee?"

"Well, there comes a time, in lots of places when the people haven't yet made up their mind that the officers ought to be pushed aside or replaced. During that time, instead of *protecting* an honest man, the laws and all the machinery are more likely to pinch the honest man's toes. Scoundrels can hide behind the law better than behind anything else. That's what we've found out. As part of the people who have a right to say what the law is, and how it's to be enforced, we had to take into our own hands the job the officers were supposed to do. In order to be law-abiding men, we put ourselves outside the book law. That's what I'm driving at."

Pat dragged smoke from his cigarette again.

"You're talking more law than most lawyers," he remarked. "And what *I* was thinking about, mostly, is that there's some in this thriving community that don't seem to be holding to any kind of law! These particular people I'm thinking about, Ross, my son, they can look at men that's not abiding by what you call book law, or what we call real law, and they can be making the finest kind of excuses for men like — well, like Kawrie, just for instance." His weathered face was inhumanly innocent under Ross's probing stare.

"Meaning which?" Ross demanded belligerently. Then, "If you're talking about Marie —" he began.

"Oh, my goodness!" Phelan protested. "And why would I be thinking about that young lady? Unless — because — maybe *you* was thinking about her?"

Ross twisted tobacco and paper into a slim cylinder, and put it into his mouth. He reached again, this time for a match from the band of his hat, and flicked it against his thumbnail. He put the tiny flame to cigarette end and smoked scowlingly before he answered.

"She's just a kid," he said at last. "In some ways she knows a lot more than girls her age. But in other ways she knows just nothing at all about — oh, about men like Kawrie."

"Or men like you?" Pat suggested softly.

"Yeh! About any kind of men," Ross nodded vigorously. "Kawrie is big and good-looking and he has the gift of gab. We don't see so many like him in this country that he ever stops being a novelty to a girl like — like Marie. He can talk a bird off a bush. And when he starts telling her why he has to do this, and that, and the other thing, that people in general misunderstand, he makes her believe it. You can't blame her! All you can do is try to show her that Kawrie is not the kind of hairpin he claims to be."

There was a soft scratching on the shuttered window of the office, followed by a low hail.

"*Adentro! Capitán!* Oh, Mr. Captain! Inside!"

Ross came to his feet and crossed the room noiselessly. Standing beside the window, he asked, "*Quien es?* Who is it?"

"One who wishes to speak to the sheriff," the man outside replied, still in Spanish. "It is important and — I do *not* wish to be seen."

"How many are there?" Ross inquired. "More than yourself?"

"But two, señor. Myself, and a trusted man of mine."

"And who are you? If you know Rayo, you should know that I do not open that door without being *very* sure that he who wishes to come in is one I wish to come in."

"I do not know Rayo. But I do wish to speak to you, and what I have to say should be most interesting and — most profitable. . . ."

"*Momentito,*" Ross told the speaker.

He turned to stare inquiringly at Pat, who was beside the shotgun now. Pat shrugged.

"With all the Blue Whistlers in this thing, I'm thinking it will be safe to let any number in up to ten," he told Ross with a grim smile.

71

"Very well," Ross said to the man outside. "I will open the door. You and your man — and you only, if there are more — will come in — each holding his ears. If you enter this room in any other way, I assure you that you will die instantly."

The man outside laughed unconcernedly.

"*Muy bien.* We will carefully hold our ears."

Ross went back to the cot and picked up a six-shooter. He cocked it, then threw the bars and pulled back the door, standing behind the shelter of its sheathing iron. Moving very deliberately, a tall, cloaked figure stepped into the room. Behind him came a smaller man.

Both were Mexicans, but very evidently of different caste. The big man in the cloak was lemon-yellow of heavy, arrogant face. He stared into Ross's eyes in the fashion of an equal. The small man — he wore no cloak, but only the cotton shirt and *pantalones* held tight to the legs by close-fitting leather leggings — was an elderly *vaquero* of lined, brown features.

Ross shut the door and dropped the bar again before he spoke. The big man grinned.

"It is permitted now that we let down our hands?" he asked. His embroidered sombrero jerked as he nodded toward Pat Phelan, now sitting upon his cot with the shotgun across his legs. The muzzle of it was trained upon the two visitors.

"But of a certainty!" Ross told him courteously. His mouth corners lifted in a thin smile. "I can see you are a man of brain. *You* would not be so ill-advised as to attempt the murder of a sheriff — with a shotgun pointed directly at you."

"For two reasons I would not," the big man agreed. "First, because Don Luis Guzmán does not commit murder. Second, because as you say, I am a man of intelligence — of *razón.* No, señor. I have come here tonight — the first time I have ever been in Rayo — to ask of you certain assistance, and to offer pay for that help I need."

He turned to the man at his elbow.

"Sit over there, Ramon," he commanded, and the grizzled little *vaquero* moved obediently, without a word in reply, to squat beside a wall.

"You are the sheriff," Guzmán said then to Ross. "Or is it another? I *heard* that the sheriff of Rayo was a man older than I."

"The high sheriff of Rayo *was* a man older than you — until this very day. Then — he died. I am the sheriff now. My name is Ross Varney."

He and Guzmán shook hands formally.

Ross waved him to a chair and Guzmán accepted it with a sweeping gesture. Ross went back to his cot and sat down. "You have heard of me, I take it?" Guzmán asked him.

Ross smiled faintly.

"Unless you are that Don Luis Guzmán of the Hacienda of the Seven Scars, I have not."

"But I *am* Don Luis Guzmán of the Hacienda of the Seven Scars!" the Mexican told him. "And — as well be frank with you — I have no right to be here, tonight. You know how our people cross your border — just as your people cross our border — with mule-trains."

"Smuggling," Ross nodded dryly.

"Well, yes," Guzmán admitted. His square face was softened by his smile. "Or — stealing. And what would you? Wherever there is a frontier there is smuggling, raiding. Always, since the world began, it has been like that. Sometimes, it is a very good thing for the people of both countries. As now, when we of Mexico need much that is made in the United States, and — it would *seem* that your merchants and traders need the *pesos* made in Mexico."

Ross shrugged.

"It's none of my affair. Being the high sheriff of Rayo County promises to keep me

74

busy until we have eight days in a week."

"But I wish this to concern you," Don Luis said — and smiled again. "I have a large train south of Skull Valley. My mules bear some thousands of *pesos.* When I enter Skull Pass, I am in your county. I need your help."

"To guard you?" Ross asked frowningly. "I can't do it. In the first place, you are dealing in contraband. You have no right to call upon me to protect you. As you have said, you have no right to be above the border. In the second place, my friend there and I *are* the sheriff's office. Two of us — no more. For you — well, I have seen too many trains like yours, not to be sure that you have armed guards to protect you against anyone you may meet on the trail."

"It is correct. Or, it is correct to some degree. I have men with rifles. But not enough. And I *know* that my train is expected; that it will be attacked."

Ross shook his head again.

"I can't help you. If you know that your train is to be attacked, why not turn back, and wait for a better time to cross the Mountains of the Skull?"

"Guzmáns do not turn back!" the Mexican said proudly. "Besides, we need the things I have come to buy. So, I will pay two thousand American dollars for your help. Surely you can hire here three or four men, to come with you and your friend?"

Again Ross shook his head stubbornly.

"It is no affair of mine, and I am in a position where, if I had three sets of hands instead of one set only, all would be well-filled. I can only counsel you to turn back, or to come forward and take your chance. But — how do you know that the train is to be attacked?"

"A man who once lived upon my estate was in Rawles."

"In Rawles?" Ross interrupted him, leaning forward a trifle, staring grimly at the heavy face.

"Yes, in Rawles. There he heard the talk in a saloon. Some spy of the outlaws in this Rawles told the leader of the thieves that my train now comes north for the first time. I have always bought from other smugglers until this time. Plans were being made to attack me in the Canyon of Skulls when this man came quietly out to meet me."

"Rawles," Ross said softly. And when he looked at Pat Phelan, his blue eyes were very dark and narrow and hard and bright.

Guzmán watched him shrewdly, seeming to understand that something about the word had weakened Ross's determination to let him go alone.

"You are — interested in this place, this Rawles?" he inquired hesitantly.

"Damned interested!" Ross assured him. "So much so that — I now give you a demonstration of a man changing his mind. I go with you, Don Luis. But not to protect smugglers! Not because of the money you offer! But because by going I strike a blow at men at whom the high sheriff of Rayo County *should* strike a blow. We two alone, my friend and I, will ride with you. There is none other in Rayo whom we can trust."

He whirled upon Pat Phelan. "Up you come, cowboy! It's back into those boots for you. Don Luis! We will ride with you within five minutes."

Guzmán stood and bowed formally. He looked shrewdly at Pat Phelan, then back to Ross.

"And I do not know of a man — two men — whom I could prefer to ride with me," he said courteously. "We will make our plans as we go, for guarding against these *ladrones* of Rawles."

CHAPTER EIGHT

The sun of mid-morning flooded the eastern slopes of Skull Mountain and arroyos and sink-holes were pools of blue shadow.

From where Ross Varney and Pat Phelan sprawled upon the stony ledge, they were sheltered from the direct rays of the sun. Jagged rocks reared above them. The spot was a mere shelf, high above that broad canyon through which a shallow stream ran. That canyon was the pass — named, because of an Indian battle of years back, "Skull Pass."

Pat stared at the fringe of willows that were green along the stream's banks. He stretched a little and flipped the butt of his cigarette down.

"I'm sort of liking the cut of that Guzmán's jumper," he said lazily. "He struck me as being much of a man — in Spanish or in English."

"Much of a man," Ross agreed.

He was looking up and down the Canyon of the Skulls. Too, he was listening. Not that he expected to hear anything in the hills behind them or on either side, but somewhere the forces of Kawrie should be assembled, if there were any truth in the tale Don Luis Guzmán had brought to Rayo.

"Pretty country," Pat Phelan said after a time. "Take that canyon down yonder. That would be my notion of the sightly place for a cow-ranch. Right yonder, that rise would be putting you out of any water that could come along, and yet you'd have the water handy. Tell you, Ross. After you clean up Rayo County, my son, why don't you resign as high sheriff, and marry somebody like — like that Marie girl! Then be going into the cow business right here."

"How would it be if you went to the edge there and jumped over?" Ross countered, without turning. "Well, I reckon Don Luis Guzmán ought to be heading this way with his train, by now."

Pat nodded and stared to the south.

"And, by the same token, I'm thinking Mr. Kawrie's merry men ought to be cavorting this way, too, coming from the other direction. Where do you reckon they would headquarter on a trip like this?"

"Well, there's a nester's place west of the Caballos, and north of here about fifteen or twenty miles," Ross answered. "Lane's place. I've heard it talked about by Long Riders, across the line. The rumor is that Lane used to be a sheriff in Wyoming. But he decided that sheriffing didn't get him rich fast enough. So he pulled out one night with all the tax-money in his *alforjas*. But, somewhere in Kansas, he bucked the tiger and dropped all his stealings. Then he came on down to Texas and hired out to some big outfit in the Panhandle as a gunfighter. But he got 'em into so much trouble, over a lot of bushwhacking he did, that he had to take it on the run. I don't *know* that he's got any connection with Kawrie's bunch or any of the other tough cases in Rayo County. But he's just the kind who would be handy for that Rawles outfit. His place would be a good hideout for 'em, if they were planning a lick at somebody in the canyon."

"How many are you reckoning will show up?" Pat asked — but without any great show of interest in his own question, or what it implied of odds against the two of them.

"Hard to say. They won't take this bunch of Guzmán's too much to heart, probably. You know how that tribe feels about a bunch of Mexican *muletaros*. They all think they can lick a dozen Mexicans apiece. Eight to ten will ride out, at a guess."

As they loitered comfortably there during the next hour, and the sun climbed toward meridian height above the mountains, Ross found himself staring across the pleasant width of Skull Canyon and viewing it, not as a possible battle-ground — which almost certainly it would become within the next three or four hours — but in the way that Pat Phelan had indicated it, as a home site.

The rise of land, like a level natural platform atop the long comb of ground that jutted out from the mountain, he could see as location for a low rambling 'dobe house. There would be ample room behind for corrals and outbuildings. And in the canyon below there was ample water for stock. . . . Even in the dry season, Skull Creek was fed by many springs of seepage water in these mountains. He nodded to himself.

"Yes, it *would* be a sightly place for a cow outfit," he thought. "And if a man had the right woman with him —"

"Bells!" Pat interrupted his thoughts of ranch — and of girl. "Well, that's sounding like the start of our little fracas, now. If the Rawles bunch will be just as accommodating, we can be getting down to business and whooping it back to town with the scalps slapping on the bridle reins."

"I hope," Ross said bodingly, "that Don Luis sticks to the plan we made. This is no time for him to get notions about a new way to fight that Rawles bunch. No time for using the old scheme, either."

He could hear the bells now, as a distant and mellow tinkling that carried far by a trick of wind in that canyon. So they waited many minutes to see the lead mule, a tiny tiger-striped animal bearing a great rawhide *aparejo.*

Then Don Luis Guzmán himself came in sight, a tall and magnificent figure, now that he had discarded his shielding cloak. He wore the traditional garb of the *charro,* the high-crowned sombrero trimmed with silver and gold, the jacket of goatskin fringed from elbow to cuff, and bright with embroidery of colored silk thread, the *chivarrias* of buckskin, close-fitting to the leg and, like the jacket, buttoned with silver.

Close behind the leader came that grizzled and taciturn *vaquero* who had trailed his master into the sheriff's office, the little man Ramon. They had one point in common beside the alertness with which they watched the canyon ahead — each held across the big horn of his saddle a new Winchester carbine.

The long train of burdened mules came in sight around a curve of the canyon. On scrubby little horses Don Luis Guzmán's retainers, seven or eight in number, guarded the flanks of the train with their rifles.

Pat Phelan sighed and shook his bristly head.

"And just to be thinking that, except for us being law-abiding men like you say we are, we could be wiping out half the bunch with our first handful of lead from here —

and running the rest of that crew with another few shots. How much, do you reckon, would Guzmán be packing in?"

"Twenty thousand; thirty thousand," Ross guessed carelessly. "I've heard of trains that packed in as high as sixty thousand in Mexican silver. But to hell with that! What I want to know is, did I guess wrong about this spot? I figured that, by the time the train got this far up the pass, Kawrie's bunch would be in sight. There's only another mile of the pass. . . ."

"Yonder, somebody's coming," Pat said curtly, with jerk of his head up the pass, in the direction of North Skull Valley. "Two men. Mexicans, too. . . ."

Ross stared at the oncoming figures. He, too, recognized them as Mexicans — by the kind of horses they rode, and the way they rode them, as well as by the tall-crowned hats which were not at first so conspicuous. Mechanically he reached behind him and picked up his Winchester. While he watched the two riders cover the distance between that elbow in the canyon and the "point" of the Guzmán train, his fingers beat a nervous tattoo upon the stock of his Winchester. He had staked a good deal on this blow at Kawrie. If Vic Lundy or some other of the tall ones in Kawrie's gang were here, it would be a very real blow. But those two men —

He watched them ride up to Guzmán. The tall Don had galloped ahead, Ramon trailing, to meet the strangers beyond the point of his mule-train. Almost below the sheltered perch of Ross and Pat the four riders halted. Guzmán's head turned toward Ramon. He seemed to say something. Ramon nodded, then lifted his hand and his shrill yell of *alto!* carried up to Ross. The men with the mules halted the animals.

"Now, what will all that pow-wowing be about?" Pat grunted.

Ross shook his head impatiently. He was very much afraid that the two were merely Mexicans riding south, and passing the train casually. Of course, they might be men friendly to their countrymen, and warning Don Luis Guzmán of an ambush farther along.

Then, as he stared, Don Luis Guzmán nodded. The gold and silver of his sombrero twinkled with the head motion. The two men who had halted him also nodded. Little Ramon was looking back toward the train.

Guzmán turned his tall, cream-colored horse, reining him about magnificently. And, as if that curvet had been a signal, a hand lifted at the side of one of those Mexicans. It came swiftly up, like a snake

84

from a hole. Ross yelled instinctively to warn Guzmán of the gun pointed at his back. But his yell could not have carried; could not have been the warning which whirled Guzmán back again. The Winchester lifted. The two shots — the assassin's and Guzmáns — blended in a single heavy report. That shabby Mexican went sideway in the saddle, clawed at his stirrup-leather for an instant, then dropped to the ground.

Ramon had been hardly less alert, and his carbine came toward the second man, now drawing a pistol with desperate clawing. But it was Pat Phelan's bullet which killed the man, a snapshot fired over the edge of the shelf.

From somewhere toward the rear of the train other shots sounded, now. Ross nodded grimly. It was very plain to him that those two riders, coming so innocently up to the head of the train, had been ordered merely to check the caravan for long enough to let Kawrie's main gang come down out of the mountains upon the guards.

When Guzmán looked up at him, Ross made a sweeping motion forward, indicating that the train was to move on. Guzmán shouted, a bull bellow of *adelante! adelante!* And with much jangling of bells, clear even above the ragged rattle of shooting from the drag of the train, the mules jumped ahead.

There were only four or five outriders — *muletaros* — now. Ross could not see, but he deduced that the others now sprawled upon the ground somewhere near the rear of the mule-train. Those who survived the volley of the outlaws lashed the mules ahead. Formation was gone. Pell-mell, jumping into a huddle, the mules galloped forward, the Guzmán *vaqueros* lashing them desperately. And at their very heels came men riding like Indians, holding rifles and carbines high, yelling savagely. They did no more shooting. Apparently they expected easily to overtake the Mexicans. There were seven or eight in all. "All right!" Ross barked at Pat Phelan. "Let's go to the party."

Calmly, now that the issue was joined, he began to shoot. . . . He missed his first man, but lowered aim a trifle and struck the man next that first target. He saw him drop from the saddle — to be swallowed up instantly in that turmoil which ensued with lashing of the outlaws by their lead.

Then the Mexicans turned, for the Rawles gang halted. Rallied by Guzmán and the little Ramon behind the galloping mules, they spread out in a thin line across the canyon. Their ragged volley poured into the enemy at short range killed horses and men alike. The ground upon which the outlaws had checked their charge was transformed into a shambles.

It was over in a twinkling. Within three minutes the yelling, enthusiastic riders had been shredded into a beaten force. The only men still in the saddle were two who had whirled their horses and now, stooping low over the saddle horn, raced back into the south. Ross fired after them, but missed.

Guzmán waved his hand and led the remnant of his retainers up to that pile of kicking horses and struggling men upon the ground. There was no more shooting; only the yells of the Guzmán side. Then two shots came from that huddle of men and animals. The great sombrero twitched upon Guzmán's head. But his men swept forward and around him and began to fire into the tragic huddle. They fired until there was no movement.

"Let's go!" Ross grunted to Pat Phelan. "This is what *I* would call a lick. I don't think Kawrie will want to talk about Skull Pass for a while — for he'll think he was licked by a bunch of Mexicans."

They scrambled up the hill to where they had left their horses and rode carefully down by the precipitous trail which had taken them to the look-out point. Guzmán rode forward to meet them as they came across the level canyon floor. His heavy face was twisted by a fierce grin. He gestured unconsciously with the carbine still gripped in his big hand.

"Beautiful!" he yelled at Ross. "It could not have been better, my friend. Those two dogs of *vaqueros* who came to get me, they thought that I was fooled when they said men waited ahead, and it would be better if I turned back. You saw one lift his hand from beneath his *chivarrias* — and what came to him when he thought to fire into the back of Don Luis Guzmán."

"I saw two get away. They were too mixed into the bunch and too far away for me to get a good look," Ross said thoughtfully. "Did your men kill all the others?"

"Every dog of them," Guzmán nodded pleasantly. "One was shooting from behind his horse, and he came near to killing me."

"I wish you'd have your men pull all of them from the horses there. It may be that, among those dead, are some whose faces I have seen."

"But yes!" Guzmán nodded.

Ramon relayed the order, then the little *segundo* and the four *muletaros* worked at the grisly business.

"They're Kawrie's men all right," Ross

told Pat Phelan. "I saw this fellow here with Kawrie in Rayo, when the gang rode up after the mob tried to take the jail. Well, as I told you a while back, I don't think Kawrie or Vic Lundy — if Vic was one of those who got away — will feel much like discussing Skull Pass for many a day."

"You're not going to be rubbing it into Kawrie about this lick?" Pat asked him curiously.

"No, I don't think so. I *may* casually mention the fact that I've heard he had a little tough luck over here. I might even say that his recruits aren't as good as they might be; that he'd better send down to the Hacienda of the Seven Scars and borrow a few men from Don Luis Guzmán."

"Look!" Pat Phelan grunted.

He jerked a big thumb toward the Don, who was standing beside a burdened mule with one of his men. They went that way and Don Luis turned with quick flash of strong, white teeth.

"I told you two thousand dollars. But I do not feel like bargaining today — not with sight of those fellows yonder before me — Here! How much can you two carry in your *alforjas?*"

"That," Pat Phelan assured him, with grin to match Guzmán's, "depends entirely,

89

amigo mio, upon *what* it is that we should carry."

Ross shook his head frowningly.

"But, as I told you in Rayo," he said, "we did this thing, not for money, but because it seemed to be what we should do as officers of Rayo County."

"Válgame dios!" Guzmán cried. "If you are so stubborn, we will not call it pay. We will call it merely a small present from a Guzmán to a Varney. We will say that I give you four or five thousand dollars, simply because today I feel like giving you that. Can there be any reason why you should not accept a present from a friend?"

"If you put it that way," Ross said smilingly, "no." He watched the silver go into their *alforjas.* Then he looked at Pat Phelan.

"Two got away," he reminded his deputy. "Now would they head for Lane's place to lick their wounds?"

Guzmán stared curiously.

"We go to find those who were not killed," Ross told him in Spanish.

"Por dios!" Guzmán grunted. "I am a hard man, but I am well content today. *I* think you are a harder man still. And — *vaya con dios, amigo!* Go with God. And when you need a friend, think of Don Luis Guzmán, of the Hacienda of the Seven Scars."

CHAPTER NINE

They rode fast, for all the burden of silver in the *alforjas*. Once out of Skull Canyon they had picked up the trail of the two fugitives and, both being trackers of the legendary type, they could ride at the slinging hard trot and see upon the hard ground of mountain and plain the tell-tale hoofmarks of their quarry.

And always the trail led due north — in the direction of that grim nester's house, Lane's. Ross grinned without mirth and Pat lifted his eyebrows inquiringly.

"Oh, everything," Ross shrugged. "In the first place, nobody in Rayo knows a thing about where we are. When the organized gang came to bang on the office door this morning, I'll bet it gave 'em a little something extra for breakfast, wondering where we went. And that little fracas in the canyon was a nice lick at Mr. Kawrie. I wouldn't say we've started out in exactly a blaze of glory, Patrick, my young and inexperienced friend. But — I do believe that you have got to make a start when and how you see the chance and we've done ex-actly that."

"If these gunnies keep on to the nester's place and wait for us to come up," Pat drawled, "we'll be doing some more of that beginning. Any notions about who they'll be?"

"Not a notion. Just a sort of hope. There's a hard case in the Kawrie gang who hefts just about as much, in my mind, as even Kawrie himself. Man named Vic Lundy. I sort of hope he'll see fit to wait for us. It would be no more than polite and it would be handy, too. I sort of want to show some of these cocksure Rayo folk that more than themselves can hold their own up and down and crossways. . . . Vic Lundy is one of the special cases I'd like to talk that over with."

"There's water ahead," Pat observed, with unnecessary jerk of the head toward the fringe of willows beyond and to the right of their course. "A creek. Not Skull Creek, either, though it might be flowing into Skull."

"Dog Creek," Ross informed him. "I have got a tolerable map of all this country in my head. I asked questions on the way up and too, I have heard a thing or two about Rayo. The man Lane has his cabin on Dog Creek. We can take that for a landmark, I think; forget the trail for the time being."

"*Muy bien,* for such rattlers as these might be thinking about somebody coming after 'em. I wouldn't put it past 'em — the way they like bushwhacking — to be lying on a

92

rock somewhere the same as we was, looking for that somebody behind. I wouldn't even be surprised if they was to shoot at us."

They cut off to the right and found the shallow creek. The trail had continued straight ahead, ignoring the water. But when Ross and Pat had ridden for perhaps two miles, they found the hoofprints of the flying riders angling to intersect their own course. Ross nodded with grim satisfaction.

"Looks like a good guess that they're for Lane's. Now we had better be slowing down a little. We might pop out into the yard of Lane's house and right into their pockets."

It was excellent judgment, for within five hundred yards the house appeared, a small flat-roofed square of 'dobe and stone, sitting in a bare stretch of ground above the creek and fifty yards from its bank. They pulled in to stare.

"Quiet," Pat observed frowningly. "And that might be meaning that our birds have flapped on by. Or —"

"I'm going to get down into the creek and ride past to have a look from the other side. If you hear shooting, you'll know I've seen something. You'll have to just use your own judgment, after that. And I hope you'll remember that you always shoot to the right too much, with a pistol. With a Winchester, I've no complaints about you. In fact" — he grinned and gathered up the reins — "I'd class you almost as good as I am."

"Yah!" Pat replied without concern, for his rifle-shooting was famous below the border. "*You* want to remember you're always after the scalplock on your man, with a Winchester, and have to be shooting twice to skin his nose."

Ross sent his horse through the willows and down into the creek. Sometimes he rode through shallow water, again upon the narrow strip of bank bordering it. Always he listened for any sound from the house. But he topped out of the arroyo among cottonwoods and willows without rousing anyone in Lane's.

The house was like a tomb in the sunlight of late afternoon. The door on this face was open but so dark was the interior that he could not make out anything within. He could not cross to the corral directly behind the house itself without being exposed to fire from doorway and narrow windows.

He studied the situation frowningly. It puzzled him that the corral was empty. That might mean that Lane nor the two they had trailed were here.

"It might," he told himself. "But between

might and *is* can be enough hot lead to sink me in the Jordan River. . . ."

But he saw nothing else to do, unless he wished to wait for darkness and that would be a couple of hours yet. He looked to the hang of his pistol, lifted his carbine into the hollow of an elbow and gathered the reins.

"When we go," he said grimly to the black, "we had better go like a bat out of hell."

He rammed in the rowels and sent the horse out of the willows in a grunting plunge. They were twenty yards into the open between creek and corral when the shot came from the house, a puff of smoke blossoming from the dusky doorway and the heavy detonation of a rifle.

The slug whined past viciously. Ross was low over the saddle horn. He did not waste time or cartridges in any attempt to answer that fire. He was concerned only in getting across the remaining forty yards or so of open ground.

The shooting became a volley. Something tapped upon the crown of his hat. He saw tiny geysers of dust rise on the ground about the black's flashing hoofs. The horse grunted as if struck but increased his speed. Ross flung himself to the ground behind the corral and inched quickly to the corner of it, carrying his Winchester.

But the heavy door slammed shut and when he fired it was to strike the planks of it only. From behind the house now came the sound of other shots.

"Pat's coming to the party," Ross nodded to himself and settled down to see what could be done. "We can thank our stars for one thing, anyway; there'll be a moon tonight and nobody can sneak out without collecting a little something to celebrate the occasion."

He put his hat on a stick and shoved it out beyond the cottonwood logs of the corral. Instantly a shot came from one of the windows and barked a log near the hat. Ross busied himself, then, with readjustment of his position. He lifted the hat over the top of the corral, still held upon the pole. But he was at the corner of the corral, carbine ready. Again the shot came; out of the same window.

He let the hat drop and sent three fast slugs into that narrow loophole in the 'dobe wall. And when he lifted the hat once more no shot came. He moved to the far side of the corral and hunted for Pat. But that seasoned warrior was not to be seen. Ross tried two shots into the other window, then moved back. There was no response.

He considered the silence without pleasure. Only one man had been indicated in the house, though two or three might have been responsible for the shooting. If only the nester was in the place, there was no legal reason for firing upon him. The fact that he had opened fire upon a rider galloping toward his house was easily explained in this neighborhood.

"In the house, there!" Ross yelled at last.

He continued to hail the place until a voice answered, a belligerent voice that carried harshly across the fifty feet to the corral.

"This is Sheriff Varney, of Rayo. Who's in there?"

"None of your damn' business!" the man told him flatly. "Sheriff or no sheriff — and I don't take no stock in that tale — you better put your tail between your laigs and make a cloud of dust getting out of here!"

"Who's doing all that loud yapping behind a wall?"

"None of your damn' business!" the man said again. "What you better be figuring on is how you can get clear. We got grub and water here. And when you come out from behind that c'ral you're going to —"

A faint, muffled explosion, like a shot fired in a closed room, cut short his sentence. Ross yelled twice again, but got no reply.

He reloaded his carbine, then stood hesitantly, scowling at the house.

"Hell!" he said irritably, and jumped into the open to sprint for the door. "If that was Pat —"

He heard shooting, now, but no lead came his way. And from somewhere behind the house Pat's voice lifted, "Watch out, Ross! Still one in there!"

But he was flattened against the wall, now, safe from any shot within the place. He moved to the door and examined it. There was no lock, merely a rawhide string that lifted a bar. And the string dangled from its hole on this side.

He jerked it and sent the heavy door swinging back with creak of rusty hinges. Someone inside fired a rifle or carbine as fast as he could work the lever and pull trigger. But Ross had not shown himself in the opening. He waited while the blast of lead came through the doorway. Then he ventured to stand a little back and to the side, and fire at an angle into the room. Two fast shots answered him then, after an interval, a third shot.

"All right, Ross!" Pat's yell came to him. "I got him!"

He heard the scuff of running feet and Pat appeared at the house corner, pugnacious face split with a wide grin. "Me, I was at the back window when you pow-wowed with the fella," he said. "I got a shot that was all he was needing. And the other one parted my hair from somewhere on the floor. I'm thinking it's safe to go in, now."

Ross looked around and found a stick of wood. He tossed it in and, when no shot greeted the thud of it on the dirt floor, shrugged and looked at Pat, then stepped into the doorway. When his eyes grew used to the gloom of the place, he found a tall man crumpled beneath the window from which the belligerent voice had come. On the floor in a corner was a second man. Both were dead.

The dirt floor was littered with brazen shells ejected from the rifles of the pair. Pat moved softly about and flung open another door, holding his pistol ready. There was a lean-to room adjoining the house and here two horses stood, saddled.

"Question is," Ross said thoughtfully, "are these our men from the canyon, or just one of 'em and the nester?"

Pat shrugged and crossed to the man under the window. He fished in pockets and brought out a shabby memorandum book.

"And this is Lane. But that wouldn't be telling that he wasn't at the canyon."

Ross went outside and studied the ground. Presently he found the trail of a single shod horse going away from the house. It was fresh enough to make him believe that two men had come to Lane's and one had stayed here, while the second rode quickly off toward Rawles. And Pat's hail from the house bore that theory out.

"This other fella, he was hit at the canyon," Pat reported. "Well, he was after being a curly wolf. Rode all that way with a bullet in his leg, then took us on when we drove up."

Ross looked over the room again and presently shrugged.

"I'm just the high sheriff of Rayo County," he said at last. "I'm damned if I'll be a grave-digger for the same pay. Let's set 'em straight and the gang from Rawles can come over and bury 'em. Some of that bunch will be along pretty soon, I reckon. If that was Vic Lundy who rode off, he'll send somebody over. It wasn't Kawrie, I know. For neither of these men was as tall as Kawrie."

They closed the door when they had unsaddled the horses and turned them out. Then they rode through the dusk back toward Rayo, making faster time than on the trip with Don Luis Guzmán. They came quietly up to the back of the sheriff's office after midnight and went to bed without seeming to rouse anyone.

"A full session," Ross said wearily. "And I'll bet tomorrow will bring another just about as crammed."

CHAPTER TEN

Ross sat up, with a Colt in each hand. He listened tensely. Someone was pounding on the heavy door of the office. Ross slipped to the floor and crossed the room, standing to one side, even though the door was iron-sheathed. A habit, this, better to preserve unbroken by an exception.

"What is it?" he demanded curtly.

"District Attorney'd like to argue with you this morning when you can get up-town," a husky voice reformed him. "Wants to look you over, I reckon."

Faintly, thereafter, came the shuffle of departing feet. Ross went over and unshuttered a window. It was the gray hour immediately before dawn, but Rayo was an early-rising community, it seemed; already there were sounds to indicate the beginning of the day's work.

"You'd better be riding out, Pat," Ross said. "Get back as soon's you can. No telling what this call from the District Attorney's all about. Well, I figured to argue with him a little, right away. Now's as good a time as any, I guess."

He saw Pat jog out of town and himself went to breakfast in a Chinese restaurant across the street. Going back, to have a look at his horse in the corral behind the jail, he was struck by something in the look of his saddle-bags. He had left the saddle hanging on a peg in the office, and subconsciously he remembered the angle at which the pockets had been tilted. It was not the same now.

"I'll be damned," he said amusedly. "Now, aren't they the busy little burglars? Certainly want to know all about me, now, don't they! Well, somebody's got a long face about now, I'd bet."

He fed the black, then went watchfully up the street and asked of a street loafer the whereabouts of the District Attorney's office. The fellow was a furtive-eyed individual and very much interested in Ross, it seemed. He kept stealing glances at the tall figure as he nodded toward the two-story adobe which was the courthouse of Rayo County.

This was enemy country, Ross thought, observing the hostile stares of those in doorways and gallery along the street. Possibly — probably — there were men who had faced the twin muzzles of the riot gun night before last. He smiled grimly at that thought and returned a level stare to everyone who looked at him.

There were two men in the District Attorney's office when Ross went in. One was an undersized, foxy-faced young man with trembling hands, who looked much like a cheap clerk in some slopshop. The other man — just then talking emphatically — was his antithesis, portly, middle-aged, dignified, with as keen and shrewd a pair of black eyes as Ross Varney had ever faced.

"I'm Varney, the sheriff," Ross said quietly. "Somebody said the District Attorney wanted to see me."

"You certainly took your time about getting here," snapped the foxy-faced man. "Meanwhile, business can wait, I suppose? Every criminal in the county would have time to ride across the Rio Grande before I could even deliver a warrant to the sheriff."

"You the District Attorney?" Ross asked unpleasantly. "Now that I figure on it, I reckon I might've known that. . . . Judging from what I've seen around here, there's not much danger of the outlaws heading for the River. I could serve almost any well-founded warrant without getting off the main street in Rayo. Glad to do it, too!"

103

"What do you mean?" snarled the District Attorney. "If you're insinuating —"

"Fellow!" Ross spoke with cold menace in face and tone alike. "Fellow, I never insinuate. It's a habit I never got into. I come right up on my feet and speak my piece — regardless! I'm telling you, now, what's straight fact. Right now, you've got the hardest looking bunch of outlaws in the country right here in your home town. From your marshal down."

"What's that?" a voice demanded from the door behind him. "What's this about from the marshal down?"

"I said" — Ross's hands slid down to the cartridge-belts about his lean waist, while the portly gentleman, silent thus far, moved swiftly to one side — "that from her city marshal down, Rayo's a nest of outlaws that needs cleaning out. And as sheriff of the county, I aim to do that cleaning. You can take that or leave it, Ellard, as you like."

Imperceptibly, he had turned, until he was facing the marshal. Ellard's colorless face was unaltered as gray stone, but his eyes shone murderously. Still, he made no move to draw.

"Here! Here!" the District Attorney cried. "You keep a civil tongue in your head while you're in my office. Rayo's doing very well with her present administration. We don't need any advice or assistance from outsiders. I sent for you to give you a warrant to serve. You take it and serve it!"

Ross took the folded paper, but merely held it in his left hand while his eyes bored into the foxy face of the District Attorney until that worthy squirmed.

"Fellow," Ross said grimly, "you take some of that advice you're so free with, and you'll find that the more doses you take, the longer you'll last. As sheriff of this county, I'm responsible for its policing and you remember one thing — there are certain crimes for which no warrant's required."

He opened the warrant, then, and with the sight of Keith Kawrie's name and, farther down, the words "highway robbery" mixed in a jumble of legal phrases, he understood a good many things about his early morning call.

"I'll bring Kawrie in today or tomorrow," he nodded, yawning artistically.

For all his careless-seeming announcement that he would bring in Kawrie within a day or two, Ross was not foolish enough to ride straight out of Rayo for the wild little community north of the county seat. He wanted to know a thing or two about Rawles, where "everything went." Disjointed remarks dropped by Yocum Nowle the night before had given him the impression that Keith Kawrie just about ran Rawles; that he reigned with a high hand over subjects any one of whom would have given an ordinary ruler much cause for thought.

He sat in the sheriff's office, Ross, with chair against the wall, boot heels hooked in a round, a brown paper cigarette drooping from his lips. His hat-brim was low over his face, and he might have been mistaken for one sleeping. But actually he was as alert as a wolf and his thoughts were racing.

So he heard a horse coming, far up the street. He did not shift his position when it halted before the office door. He heard the rider swing down and then recognized Pat Phelan's rolling step.

"Ball's rolling," Pat announced happily. "Anybody around? Well! Inside a week, Ross, me laddie-buck, we'll be having ten-twelve of the saltiest cowboys even this neck of the woods has ever rested peevish eyes upon. We will that!"

"I've got a job," Ross said absently. "I'm riding over to the wild and woolly camp of Rawles. . . . Yep! Got a warrant for Keith Kawrie. Highway robbery. Seems he was getting skinned in a monte game, so he stuck up the dealer and scooped in the money regardless."

"And what'll be beyond this job?" Pat inquired shrewdly. "Sure, she's not a simple matter of serving a warrant, then?"

"She's not! She's just a move to see how easy I can be killed off. It's a one-man job, Pat, old-timer, but — Tell you what! Rawles is about a dozen miles north. I wish you'd trail me without letting yourself be seen leaving Rayo. Pick a good place about half way between here and there and wait for me. Maybe I'll be pretty glad to have a little company coming home."

"I will that!" Pat nodded grimly. "Sure, if you go sticking your head into that camp, asking the man Kawrie will he *please* to come along and mebbe be taking a trip to jail, you'll be apt to be needing lots of company home!"

"I'm going to wander a little and mingle with somebody who knows about Rawles," Ross grunted, heedless of Pat's gloomy face.

At the door he paused, to turn and grin at his lieutenant.

"I'm thinking that if I need you, Pat, in town, the signal will be a whole corralful of pistol shots!"

He loafed up the street, studying the men he met. It occurred to him that of all these who passed and re-passed, a good many were honest, trustworthy. But, so far as he was concerned, every one of them might as well be an avowed outlaw, for he was a stranger to them all. More and more it was being conveyed to him that his handicap as sheriff of a county wholly strange to him was a weighty one indeed. But he was not one to worry unduly. He whistled a little under his breath, very cheerfully.

"Here comes that heavy-set hairpin who was in the District Attorney's office," he said suddenly to himself. "Wonder who he was? He was laying down the law about something when I walked in."

When he came abreast of the portly gentleman, who wore the "planter's" Stetson and frock coat, both of somber black, that usually mark a lawyer, he was surprised a little to be greeted with a genial smile.

"How do you do, Mr. Sheriff," said the portly gentleman. "There was — ah — no opportunity for introductions in Irlan's office a while ago. But I am Judge Xavier."

"Glad to meet you — officially," Ross grinned. "For in this county, it surely looks as if all three of us honest *hombres* ought to stick together! If our mutual acquaintance, Mr. Ford Irlan, is not a .22-caliber crook under the marshal's thumb, then I'm a Chinese pot-walloper — the which I'm not."

The judge grinned in return, nor seemed to care particularly that Ross expressed an opinion so painfully low of Mr. Irlan who, as District Attorney, was in some wise the judge's colleague.

"You're not a Blue Ribboner, I trust?" was his hospitable reply. "Fine! Then let's adjourn to Mr. O'Donnell's establishment, here. There are some comfortable tables in the rear — set thoughtfully far apart — and I have initiated Mr. O'Donnell into the sacred mysteries of a recipe of my own. It's named 'The Sunrise Highball.' But don't let that deter you; *my* Sunrises are guaranteed to function at any hour of the day."

He led the way into the long saloon of Mr. O'Donnell and nodded to men here and there as they progressed toward the tables — set so thoughtfully far apart — in the rear. The table he selected was in a corner, where one might sit with back comfortably and strategically against the angle of two walls, and thus observe the room with but his face exposed.

"You — have the warrant for Kawrie?" Xavier drawled, in a tone that could not have carried six feet. "You intend to serve it, of course? . . ."

"Oh, yes," Ross nodded. "But don't think for a minute that I don't understand why

I'm sent after Keith Kawrie."

"When are you going to Rawles?"

"*Muy pronto.* But I've heard a thing or two about that camp, and I'd like to get a handful more of the horrible details before I go horning in."

"Of course; of course! Well, perhaps I can help. Rawles is just a supply camp for the cattle-ranchers around. Some of the Rayo mining companies have claims in that neighborhood, but they aren't working them. The population is chiefly floating — except for Kawrie's gang. Perhaps you already know that, as a gunfighter, Kawrie is very much Vic Lundy's inferior? I assure you that he is. Vic, incidentally, has killed four men in the past nine or ten months. Three of them he got with the gun he carried in a quick-draw shoulder-holster."

"And the other?"

"With a sawed-off shotgun — the shotgun of one of Ellard's deputies. You see, the deputy got the drop on Vic, but let him get too close. Vic caught the gun and pulled it away from the deputy. Blew him in two with it. . . ."

Ross looked with deepening regard at the courtly figure opposite him. Nor was the warmth he felt for Judge Xavier due to the mellow, golden drink he was sipping. The judge might have told him facts about Rawles, facts true enough, but not particularly helpful. But when he dwelt upon such points as Kawrie's caliber as a gunman. Vic Lundy's habits with the Colts, he proved to Ross's entire satisfaction that he was really friendly.

"With it all," the judge went on thoughtfully, "Vic is by no means without sterling qualities. I have never heard of him betraying a friend, and, personally, he is quite likable. But — one had best cultivate his friendship before asking a favor. . . ."

"Which leaves me where? I'm figuring to bring Kawrie back with me, regardless. This is one detail I'm surely going to fill. If ever I get close enough to Kawrie to throw a gun on him, without anybody coming in between us, nobody's going to take him away from me. Not alive, that is. . . ."

"You may have to employ that method. But I should advise telling him frankly why you've come and — well, stressing the fact that it will boost Ellard's stocks if the county officers can't serve warrants. As to obtaining bail — well, we're perhaps a bit looser than is good, hereabout, in granting bail; almost as bad as a large city. I can't make any promises about granting bail, now, but — tell Kawrie you talked to me."

"Thanks!" Ross said, earnestly, getting up. "But I'm sort of sorry about this bail business. I'd like it lots better if there was some way to keep the fellows in there after I slam the door on 'em. You reckon things'll change in that line?"

"Why —" the judge's black eyes twinkled as he held up the "Sunrise" and studied it critically — "there has really been no valid objection on the part of either — faction, shall I say? I have at least tried to be impartial, seeing little to choose between the two factions. But if, after observation, I see anything to be gained by refusing bail in any or all cases — Trot to Rawles, Varney, and get your man. Hereafter, you can be assured that you'll get all the legitimate support in the world from the District Judge."

Ross nodded, went out and back to the jail. Pat was not in sight and so Ross saddled the black and cut through the outlying part of town to reach the Rawles road. In a doorway he saw Ellard standing, watching him with pale face impassive as usual. On impulse, Ross moved his horse so that he rode close to the doorway.

"Going after Keith Kawrie, huh?" Ellard inquired.

"Why, certainly!" Ross nodded, face mirroring surprise. "You see, I'm packing a warrant for him."

"Reckon I'll have time to get a bite to eat, before you come back with him?" the marshal inquired. Ostentatiously he consulted his watch. "Or had I better get right down to the courthouse to see you fetch him in?"

"Depends on how long you take to eat. But you can wait at the courthouse all right — dead sure we'll meet you there, fellow. For I'm coming back from Rawles. Yes, sir! I'll be at the courthouse. I'll be there with my hair in a braid!"

Chapter Eleven

Uphill, downhill, skirting the mines and climbing the ridges beyond, so the yellow-white road curved lazily toward Rawles. Ross rode thoughtfully and when he came to a slope covered with great red boulders, surmounted by an old deserted cabin and somewhat dilapidated log corral, he hoped that Pat Phelan would see the strategic possibilities of this location, half way between Rayo and Rawles as it was.

He built another cigarette and lounged in the Texas saddle with one leg crooked about the horn, whistling, staring thoughtfully upward at the fleets of snowy cumulus cloud which floated over a serene blue southwestern sky. He was thinking of Marie Nowles.

What a girl . . . what a girl! He had never encountered one even remotely like her, quick-witted, courageous, yet utterly girlish, too. The fleecy clouds above his head began to alter and shift in his mind's eye, piling into Castles of Spain.

"I'm in a hell of a situation!" Ross told himself. "Hadn't been for Mig' Mora's bushwhacking the Big Boss, I'd be sole owner of a real cow-ranch, and I'd be wearing the brand of that college. And instead, here I sit you, you blamed black billygoat. I'm twenty-three years old, owning just what we cover from the ground up. Still, if it hadn't been for Mig's killing Dad, I wouldn't have met her . . . Marie Nowle. Marie. . . ."

There was an interruption to his chain of thought when he sighted a weathered adobe ranch house over on a western slope, perhaps a mile off the trail. From behind it showed a cloud of yellow dust, slow-rising in the still air. Ross stared at this evidence of men working, then he shrugged and turned the black toward the house.

"Might's well get acquainted with this neighborhood," he told himself. "It'll maybe pay dividends to know everybody between

Rayo and Rawles."

He had covered perhaps two-thirds of the distance to the house when an extraordinarily tall man appeared on the front gallery to lift his hands to his eyes. For a moment Ross was puzzled, then he saw that the tall man was studying him through a pair of glasses. He grinned at this evidence of suspicion. It seemed very characteristic of Rayo County's state of mind. Evidently, he thought, the tall man had not been unduly alarmed, for he set the glasses down and stepped back inside the doorway which showed as a black rectangle behind him.

But when the man reappeared almost instantaneously and lifted a rifle, when a tiny smoke-puff blossomed at the weapon's muzzle and a bullet sang over his head, Ross changed his opinion. He changed his posture at the same moment, moving with the instinctive speed and precision of a man who has been shot at before. When the black was sheltered behind a huge boulder, Ross loosened his Winchester carbine in its scabbard and peered around the side of the great rock.

The altered color of the doorway rectangle told Ross that the door itself was now closed. He drew the carbine and scowled at the gray building. There was the faintest suggestion of movement in an unshuttered window to the right of the doorway and Ross, taking careful aim and steadying himself against the boulder, drove two bullets into the window.

His shot was answered swiftly from one side of the house. He dismounted and dropped flat upon the ground. Then, taking advantage of every mesquite and greasewood bush, of such shelter as was afforded by small boulders, he moved like an Apache toward the house from which he had been fired upon.

"Somebody's up to something," he thought grimly. "And if they're not, they're going to learn it's not the healthiest thing in the world to be slamming lead at every stranger that comes along. Specially when that stranger is the lawfully appointed sheriff of that damn' county!"

Fortunately, there was no ridge near the house, behind which the men there could slip down toward the great boulder sheltering his horse. So they must take it for granted that he was still there. They had not detected his advance — he was sure of this by reason of the absence of any bullets heading toward him. So he inched forward, as many a time he had slipped up to capture

the Mexican herders and *vaqueros* of Mig'
Mora.

Masked by a greasewood bush, he studied
the house from a squatting position with
carbine upon his knees. Something moved
at a corner. He drew back a little and lifted
the Winchester, waiting. And out from the
edge of the house came half the face of a
man, his right shoulder point. It was hardly
more than seventy-five yards and Ross's
elbow was steadied upon his knee. At the
shot, the man fell sideways, into plain sight.
An arm lifted jerkily, fell, was not lifted
again. The man lay still.

From the windows of the house and from
the corner came a hail of bullets. Ross had
dropped flat the moment he had pressed
the trigger. Most of the lead whined spitefully above him; some plowed the dust
uncomfortably close by. But after a couple
of minutes he began his snail-like advance
again, grinning as he reflected that the bullets which still searched through the greasewood were higher and higher above his head
as he crept and wriggled nearer the source
of fire.

A boulder gave him beautiful cover from
which to study the other side. Three men
were firing and he watched the house corner, as the point from which a man firing

was most exposed. When he was sure of his aim he had but to wait for a shoulder to show, then drive a .44 through it. That left two — that he knew about.

Came now a perfect rain of bullets against the boulder that walled him in. He ducked low, but even so splinters of rock stug his scalp like sleet. They were alternating on him, he guessed, taking turns at loading and firing. And the very steadiness of the fire, the way it was focused on the stone in front of him, suddenly gave him warning.

Squinting his eyes against rock chips, he craned his neck to look upward almost from the very ground. Two men were coming toward him, no more than fifty feet away, coming at a crouching run. They advanced time about, one firing, the other moving. Ross discarded his carbine for the handier Colt. A bullet rapped the boulder almost in his face as he flipped the hammer back and let drive at the tall man who had fired the first shot of this battle. The ringing of the lead on stone deafened him; involuntarily he shut his eyes. When he opened them again, the tall man was sprawling loosely, face down.

The other man had stopped shooting for an instant. He blazed away swiftly as Ross stood up like a Jack-in-the-box, but the bullet went wild. Ross's did not. He fired twice from the hip — right hand, left hand. Puffs of dust rose from the fellow's flannel shirt, as from a beaten rug. Ross darted forward and kicked the dropped rifle out of reach, but there was no need.

He squatted beside the pair and his eyes flashed from them to the house and back again. Up there, all was quiet. He could see the first man he had shot lying at the house-corner. But the one caught in the shoulder had crawled back out of sight. Bent low, Ross ran for the gallery. There was no shot from the house as he came. His hat was hanging down the back of his neck by its chin-thong. Squatting close against the house-wall, inside the gallery, he got the hat off and hurled it at a window. In the same instant he sprang inside the door.

A man was prone on the floor inside, weakly holding up a Colt with both hands, training it on the window. He tried to shift his aim to Ross, but groaned with the movement.

"Drop it!" Ross snarled. "Drop it, or I'll drill you!"

"You got me!" wheezed the man on the floor. He let the Colt go. "But, stranger, I'd sure like to know who'n hell you are!"

"Varney, Sheriff of Rayo County!"

119

"Then Orval Quett was right! He says you looked a heap like the new sheriff. He saw you in town yesterday."

"That's why he shot over my head, was it?"

"Hell, no! He was trying to get you plumb center. But Orval, he never could do more'n just shake the loads out of a Winchester."

"Well!" Ross drawled, forethoughtedly raking the Colt out of the fellow's reach with boot-toe, "you're surely a cheerful bunch of bushwhackers, now aren't you? Here I come riding up all peaceful and your man Orval starts to part my hair for me!"

"Was those Flying-X horses out back," the man grinned, sitting up and nursing his wounded shoulder tenderly. "Orval and Emory Glass and Wesley Jannett, they weren't specially wanting any visitors today. Me, I'm not in the deal at all. Just happened to be here when you rode up and of course, I had to take a hand in the shooting — like a damn' fool."

"Oh-ho! Stolen horses, huh? Funny — I just came from Rayo and nobody there said anything about having horses stolen."

"No time," grinned the cheerful partisan. "But when Judge Xavier and Curt Prentiss do get the word from their foreman — well, you'll likely hear a heap."

"Wonder if I can haze 'em by myself," Ross pondered aloud. "You'll have to go back with me, of course. Maybe you didn't help rustle this stuff, but that's for the judge and jury to decide. Reckon I'll have to call you an accessory after the fact, if nothing else."

"You're sure going to land law and order into this county with both barrels, now aren't you?" breathed the man on the floor. "What for a fancy business is this accessory stuff? Either a fellow swings the long rope or he don't. You can't hang nothing on me just because I chanced to come along right after Orval and the others ran off the Judge's thoroughbreds."

"The hell I can't," Ross disputed him grimly, though with no particular unfriendliness for this reckless cowboy in his bearing. "Listen, fellow! I aim to put a complete stop to all varieties of crime in this county. I'll land the fellows that pulled the job and I'll bring their friends along for good measure.

"From now on, a man's going to be out in the open on one side or other — he's going to not only mind the law, but he's going to back it. Else he's going to wear the outlaw iron on his left hip. The fellow that stands in with a crooked bunch is just as bad as they are, and he's going to be treated as such."

"How long do you think you'll last, to put your fancy ideas on this country's hide?" jeered the cowboy. "You've bucked up to Ellard — that's enough to wipe out your mark. But the minute you come bothering around Keith Kawrie or Vic Lundy, you better bring along a nice little old tag, addressed to whoever you'd like to have your remains."

He fished out tobacco and papers and built a cigarette, grinning the while. He jerked a match from his hatband, lighted his smoke and got awkwardly to his feet.

"Come on, Sheriff!" he grinned palely. "This damn' arm you perforated is beginning to get me shaky. Let's hightail it for Rayo. I want to fix it up about my bond."

"Things are changing a little that way, too," Ross drawled maliciously. "Maybe you won't be let out on bond. Come along, fellow. I reckon you're all right, by your lights. Trouble with you is, since yesterday you've sort of been out of date."

He motioned the prisoner toward the back of the house and so they came to the corral. One glance at the rangy horse band inside was evidence enough to have convicted Orval and his co-workers in any rangeland court, for five of the twenty-three animals had their original Flying-X brands altered to Cross-in-a-Box. Evidently it had been the dust raised in the work of brand-blotting which Ross had seen from the trail.

Fortunately the horses were weary. Ross let down the gate-bars of the corral and, with some yelling and hat waving, got the band outside, where they ran for a little way, then stopped.

"Get your horse," he ordered the prisoner. "We're going back to that old cabin a couple of miles back."

When the cowboy was mounted Ross headed the stolen animals toward the corral and they jogged along tamely enough. Ross wondered if Pat would be waiting at the cabin. There was a chance, of course, that he would have come past it and be somewhere on the trail to Rawles. In that case, he must take the horses and prisoner to Rayo.

But as the horses stopped near the rickety corral, Pat appeared in the cabin's door. He grinned and shifted his carbine to the crook of his arm, then came out.

"Sure, you look amazing like a young fellow getting a start for himself!" he cried. Then, as he saw the blotted brands, his small blue eyes narrowed and he regarded

the grinning cowboy thoughtfully. *"You —
do — that!"* he grunted in changed tone.

"Let's get 'em into the corral," Ross said
impatiently. "You'll stay here with 'em, and
ride herd on our young friend here, until I
come back. He claims that he didn't do the
actual stealing, but he certainly cut down
on me like a willing soul when I came up to
mingle with his friends. So I had to do a
little operation on him. He had three friends
in the sticky rope line and I needed one for
a witness, so I saved him."

They drove the horses inside the gateway.
Pat took the lariat from the silent prisoner's
saddle, to stretch across the gateless gap.
He looked about him uncertainly for a moment, then went back to the cowboy, to
twitch the green neckerchief from his throat.

"Hey!" protested the robbed one. "Just a
minute! Just because you got me with my
pants down, like this, ain't no reason to steal
the clothes off me! That doll rag took five
round, silver dollars out of the old family
fortune."

"Hush, my child!" Pat adjured him pa-
tiently. "Sure, we'd have to take it off you,
anyway, when we come to hang you."

He knotted it on the lariat to flap and keep
the horses back, then looked significantly at
Ross, who took the hint.

"Pile off," he grunted to the prisoner. "Inside with you and don't try anything that might get you killed."

Then he looked inquiringly at Pat, who was humming beneath his breath.

"Sure you've heard about El Tecolote arriving?" was Pat's broadside. "Shh! The word's traveling the town over by now. Yeh. El Tecolote stuck up the west-bound stage yesterday beyond Rayo and walked off with the better part of four thousand dollars, Ross, my son. . . ."

"Now, who thought of that?" Ross breathed. "Pat, we're going to have a little detective work to do, I reckon, just to fill the gaps in our working time. There's somebody from down south in this country. I wonder if it *could* be somebody we know. Yes, sir! I wonder. . . ."

"Can happen! Sure, in tromping the toes of Mig' Mora, we may well have trod a few corns of which we took small heed at the moment. Well, she's of small moment at this time. You'll be going on to Rawles?"

Ross was walking back to his horse, near the door. He nodded.

"I'm going on to Rawles now. Wait here for me. I'll bring Kawrie back tomorrow morning likely. May have to tote a few of his hired help too."

"So you're going to Rawles and fetch back Keith Kawrie and some of the boys, just like that!" their prisoner cried, grinning. "Oh, my gosh! And me and this deputy, *we* have got to wait till you get back with 'em! I'll write in and see if I can't stake out this land. I'll have it proved up on, easy, before you get back."

"See you some more, Pat," Ross said evenly, ignoring the jibes. "Don't kill this hairpin — unless you happen to feel like it."

Chapter Twelve

In the few remaining miles that separated him from Rawles and whatever might lie in wait there for him, Ross passed four or five riders who eyed him aslant, nodded very gravely, stared thoughtfully at his long-limbed black, and fox-trotted past him. Men of varying ages, from twenty, perhaps, to forty, were these, but whatever their years might number, they were alike in the careless roughness of their clothing, in a certain grim watchfulness and wolfish alertness of bearing. Alike were they, also, in that each wore sagging at his side either one or two long-barreled Colts, and that each crooked a leg over the scabbard of a saddle Winchester.

126

"A salty country!" Ross told himself. "A salty country — by God!"

With that reflection his mouth tightened, and his blue eyes took on the hard, dull glint they had worn when, in the full expectation of instant death at Rayo jail door, he had extended his chill invitation to come on.

The yellowish trail crooked and curved as the whims of its red makers had dictated in the beginning, around mesquite clumps and through greasewood brush, until it became the single expansive "street" of Rawles. Ross reined in upon the edge of the little camp and slowly a corner of his thin mouth lifted as he surveyed the twin, straggling rows of unpainted plank or graying log buildings.

Horses stood thick along the hitch-racks this morning. Men sat or squatted on unroofed plank verandas and talked and waved their hands. Fifty or sixty men, he could see, walking or standing or sitting so. Evidently, he decided, he had come at a time when an audience was assured him. He made a little gesture full of resignation, half-humorous, half-grim, then tickled the black with a rowel and rode on.

At the first saloon he pushed his mount in between two tied ponies, swung down and hitched the black, then ducked under the hitch-rack and stood looking thoughtfully about. Twenty or thirty pairs of eyes — and whether black or gray or blue or brown or hazel, these eyes owned in common a curious alertness — were upon him.

"Howdy!" Ross nodded colorlessly to the nearest man. "Where's Keith Kawrie?"

"In there," the man addressed said slowly. "Who're you? What do you want of Keith?"

Ross eyed him steadily, then laughed and pushed on by. As he neared the door of the place indicated as Kawrie's whereabouts, he could hear the man's angry mumble behind and the sound of low laughter from others. He went on in.

The place was a long shed-like room, its rafters canopied, just now, with blue smoke haze from pipe and cigarette. Ten or twelve men were there, either at a long pine bar that extended the room's length, or playing cards at rude tables here and there. Over in a corner was a very long man upon a small box; his gaunt knees were almost under his chin; the tails of a rusty ministerial-looking frockcoat flapped all about him. He was like a clothes-pole upon which the coat had been hung carelessly.

Ross, in the act of looking about for Keith Kawrie, was attracted by this man — who was apparently absorbed in a small black volume which he held up close to his face.

But after an instant, as he stared, Ross saw the book stealthily lowered and above it, between its top and the brim of a dusty black Stetson the man wore low upon his forehead, appeared a hatchet face with pale eyes close set, boring into the new-comer.

"Hallo!" cried Keith Kawrie from a table in the room's rear, behind which he was slumped out comfortably. "How is our High Sheriff today? Is this a — social call?"

Ross grinned slowly. He went back toward Kawrie. It both amused him and most accurately established the caliber of this savage community, when he noted how each man there, save only Kawrie, was suddenly in such position that his hands nestled very close to his weapons.

There was a soap-box beside the table at which sat Kawrie and three others, Vic Lundy one of them, playing poker. Ross pulled up the box and seated himself comfortably. Kawrie watched him sidelong, with a small, sardonic smile, to match Ross's own. Vic Lundy eyed Ross with some curiosity, but without any appearance of tension such as the two other players manifested.

"So you accepted my invitation?" Kawrie drawled. Then, to Vic Lundy, "I said I'd raise you five."

"I said I'd be over. Only thing is, I came a little sooner than I figured."

Kawrie cocked his head sideways and surveyed his hand as if nothing else in the world were of real importance. Ross, studying anew the dark, handsome face, with its broad forehead and thin-lipped mouth, again realized that here was no ordinary "hard case." The good blood in Kawrie which had given him his position here, made him more dangerous, because more brainy, than if he had been — say, Vic Lundy.

"Civil business?" Kawrie inquired, turning back to Ross after a moment.

"Um — well, I'm afraid not," Ross shrugged, as he made a cigarette. "Fact is, the business is pretty un-civil, but I try to act civil, no matter what the business may be."

He fished a match from his hatband, scratched it, set it to the end of his cigarette and watched a curl of smoke go slowly to become part of the canopy about the rafters.

"I took the job of sheriffing sort of blind," he drawled. "I told you in Rayo that there looked to me to be a lot of cross-patch, crazy-quilt politics that I couldn't exactly figure. It's sort of funny how the High Sheriff of Rayo County has to be on the outs with the town authorities. Ellard and I will be shooting it out one day soon, no doubt of that. But meanwhile, he's standing in with that little crook Irlan, and Irlan, he hands me warrants to serve. . . ."

Kawrie still seemed hardly interested; or, at least, more interested in his cards than in what Ross was saying. But Vic Lundy, evidently a man faster with his twin Colts than at thinking, scowled a little perplexedly. Ross regarded his cigarette thoughtfully.

"Irlan gave me a warrant this morning — for you, Kawrie. Highway robbery. That business about the monte game in Vado a couple of weeks ago."

"Funny!" Kawrie drawled, as if the warrant and charge concerned someone else. "Man starts in a monte game and discovers that the deck's been stripped of his 'hunch' cards. He's lost three or four hundred and so he retorts to the — ah — *fundamental,* to recover what he's been cheated of. And the gambler swears out a warrant! Vic, this country is getting too damn' civilized for us; too much like back East!"

"I — I have an idea the monte dealer maybe wouldn't have done more than squawk," Ross grinned, "if it hadn't been for you being short in Rayo with the Law and Order gang. Ellard and Irlan figure that

131

this is a sort of double-barreled gun, this warrant: it's figured to cause trouble for you and me both, Kawrie. And, too, it has still another sharp point.

"By what I hear, you have always sort of backed the county officers — for your own private reasons, of course, and just to be against the towners. Now, they want to see if you're going to be let alone by me. That would be a good excuse for calling me a Kawrie-man."

"What do you intend to do about the warrant?" inquired Kawrie, still without looking at Ross.

"Serve it, of course! I figure to serve every warrant I get. But this particular charge is what I called it — just a way to raise hell between you and me. So I spoke to Judge Xavier about your getting bail. And I know that there won't be any towners horning in on the business. You'll go with me and anybody who tried to start anything'll surely meet trouble. And meet it in the smoke."

"And if I — I don't choose to accept service of the warrant?" Kawrie asked very softly.

Vic Lundy's hands were out of sight under the table. So were those of his two companions. Vic's hard, black-stubbled face was softened by a wide grin of purest amusement — but Ross had no illusions born of this. At the word, he felt that Vic would open fire on him and kill him with the humorous twinkle still lighting his small black eyes.

His own hands were jammed into trousers pockets. He grinned at Kawrie sardonically.

"Why, if you don't want to play with me, and walk into Rayo and worry the Ellard outfit that way, it will just mean I never will float again — too many holes in me and too much lead. But, when the smoke blows away in here, there'll be three of us on the floor — you, and Vic there, and Yours Truly. Even if Vic gets me with that .45 he's holding under the table, this derringer in my right pocket will settle his coffee. The one in my left pocket, of course, will be yours, Keith. . . ."

Vic scowled uncertainly. Keith Kawrie showed his emotions by no more than a narrowing of full-lidded black eyes. The other pair of poker players were obviously puzzled and waiting for leadership. What was going on behind him Ross could not say, but he was alert for the first tiny sound of footsteps approaching his back.

Suddenly Kawrie laughed and raised both his hands in a mocking gesture. And Ross, watching with painful intentness, decided that the precipice was skirted — for this moment.

"In that case, I'll go with you," Kawrie nodded. "Yes, this time I'll go with you for the reasons you mentioned, and for certain others I hold privately. I'll go — this time."

"Fair enough!" Ross grinned. "If ever I have to come after you again, it'll be a fair deal, Kawrie: you can always make up your mind what you want to do."

"We'll go this afternoon. Meanwhile you might as well get acquainted with the prominent members of our citizenry. As I told you when I invited you to come to Rawles, they're a very energetic, business-like sort. I assure you that they all are deeply interested in you already. They'll be very glad to meet you."

He got up abruptly. Ross, Vic and the others stood also. Kawrie glanced about the bar-room, and at sight of the tall hatchet-faced man in the frockcoat — he who seemed so engrossed in the black-bound book — his eyes twinkled.

"Flint!" he called. "Oh, Isidor! Come shake hands with the High Sheriff of Rayo County!"

Flint got up with a flopping of ungainly limbs that made him seem like a shaken jumping-jack. Ross, looking into the pale, close-set eyes, the thin, hollow-cheeked face, felt an instinctive repulsion, as strong as if he stared into a rattler's sinister eyes. He had no warning of the day to come when he would search for this Isidor Flint with hot determination to kill, but still his hand shrank in the damp, cold grasp of the man.

"Isidor," Keith Kawrie told him mockingly, "represents the Moral Aspiration of Rawles. Or so he says. He is greatly pained by the small lapses from propriety of our more exuberant youngsters. In the delivery of admonitory lectures, he is our outstanding example. You observed, of course, that while the rest of us were engaged in card-playing and other wicked devices, Isidor was deeply engrossed in that pious-seeming book."

"Which is," Ross remarked with a slight, contemptuous smile, "an unusual sort of book . . . Boccaccio in a black morocco binding like a book of sermons."

Flint popped the volume in question into some pocket beneath his coat. He shook his head sadly at Ross. "My friends," he said in the nasal twang of the professional exhorter, "how can the ignorant rebuke sin? Ain't it necessary that them that aspires to curb the carnal instincts in their fellow man should know the paths by which men tread toward the flames? Assuredly, my friend!"

Ross's contemptuous grin widened. He turned his back upon Flint to look over the others. Kawrie led him toward the door, giving one outlandish nickname after another in introducing those who, grinning, stuck out grimy paws to meet the sheriff's.

"Glad to meet you, Sheriff!" they told Ross humorously. "Glad to meet you this way, and hope we always stay friends!"

Chapter Thirteen

It was the same on the street. Ross felt himself somewhat at cross-purposes. Outlaws these men were; some were cold-faced killers. But, in the main, they were what they were without pretense. About their very crimes there was a rugged sincerity a man must admire. Isidor Flints with sanctimonious smirks were almost unknown among such as made the evil fame of Rawles in that country.

Not that the admission meant any slackening in his quiet fixity of purpose. As sheriff, he might agree that Vic Lundy, for instance, owned many a trait that a man wanted in his friends. But when Vic stepped outside the rangeland law and the warrants went out, Ross would serve them, would face Vic through the smoke and over long black barrels, or knot the hangman's noose without weakening caused by memory of friendly drinks they might have had together.

Keith Kawrie disappeared. He said that he had a detail or two to settle before leaving Rawles for the county seat. Vic Lundy took the post of guide and conductor. He and Ross finally sat down at a table in another saloon and formally pledged each other's health in bright amber whisky from the proprietor's last barrel.

"What's this about the border *hombre,* this El Tecolote, sticking up the stage?" Ross asked carelessly over their second drink.

"Don't know," Vic shrugged. "Wonder if those damn' wagons never are coming; camp'll be out of liquor pretty soon, if they don't get here."

"Happened since I left town," Ross continued. "Funny that a hairpin like El Tecolote would drift into Rayo County and start off on his own, without trying to hook up with Ellard's outfit — or somebody up this way."

His frank grin robbed the allusion to Vic's friends of offense. The squat gunman grinned in turn.

"Can't tell about those fellows," he drawled. "You're — right interested in this

137

fellow, huh?"

"Of course! I sort of like to know the hairpins I'm likely to be swapping lead with, before we start the ball rolling."

"I haven't been in Rayo to hear about the stage getting stuck up," Vic remarked, with more blandness than Ross had given him credit for possessing. "Maybe Keith knows something about it."

"Can happen," Ross said dryly. Vic's small eyes twinkled at his tone.

They sat staring at their full glasses and Ross wondered if that crime, and the placing of responsibility upon the shoulders of El Tecolote, had been a thing of Rayo, or of Rawles; of someone in Ellard's following, or a member of Keith Kawrie's outfit. He thought, with a slow smoldering of anger more dangerous than any swift outburst of fury, that he would give almost anything to know the truth.

Vic's back was to the street door of the place; Ross, sitting opposite him, faced it. At the click of high-heeled boots upon the plank floor he raised his eyes mechanically and would have rubbed them bewilderedly had there been time. For bearing down upon their table was the double of that tall horse-thief, Orval Quett — whom he had dropped that morning.

One of Ross's hands, the left, was on the table, touching his whisky glass. His right was jammed into a trousers pocket. The tall man, his face a mask of rage, came stalking up, long, clawlike hands brushing the butts of his Colts. Vic, hearing him approach, turned with a swift wriggle like a wolf's, hands going glidingly to his lap.

"Hi-yah, Greaser!" he greeted the newcomer.

"Y'all the sher'ff?" snarled "Greaser" to Ross, deaf to Vic's greeting. Then, as Ross nodded and Vic stared from one to the other of them, Greaser bent slightly over the table.

"Yuh downed my brother, Orval, this morning! An' I'm downin' you this afternoon!"

Vic's black eyes flashed from Greaser to Ross, seeming to investigate the position of Ross's hand. Unobtrusively he moved his stool backward until he was well out of line of their probable fire.

"So Orval was your brother," Ross drawled thoughtfully. "Well, now that I look you over, I do see a sort of family likeness. Twins, were you?"

He could not get his hand out of trousers pocket without an abrupt movement that Greaser would see; his left hand on the table was awkwardly far from a weapon, while

Greaser's hand crept up to his crossed belts, no more than an inch or so each from the low-swung Colts he wore. No doubt about it, this lank avenger had him foul. Desperately he played for time, for some diversion.

"Yes, we was twins!" Greaser snarled ferociously. "Yuh downed him an' now I'm goin' to take your hair, yuh — yuh —"

"Sh!" Ross said imperatively. "First thing you know, fellow, you'll be giving yourself away. Orval was absent-minded, sort of, about horses and the like. He'd start out rounding 'em, you see, and clean forget about just looking for his own brand. That's something many a fellow's got snarled up over. Now you surely don't want to give yourself out as being the same sort of hairpin."

"I — I —" began Greaser. Apparently Ross's manner puzzled him. Certainly it had delayed the climax that he had stalked inside the saloon to bring out.

"Anyhow, he cut down on me with a Winchester," Ross cried angrily. "What kind of a family is yours anyhow? Man can't be riding along quiet and peaceful without one of you coming out of some hole a mile away and cracking down on him. Why, why, the fellow might have *hit* me!"

He picked up the glass of whisky and

glared at Greaser Quett.

"Yuh think you're damn' smart, now don't you!" Greaser roared furiously, seeming to realize the tenor of the talk for the first time. *"I'll show yuh!"*

His hands twisted; slipped around the Colt butts; lifted. And squarely into his eyes Ross flung the whisky, then sent the table crashing sideways with a sudden thrust of his knee; took one step forward and drove a hard left fist to the point of the other's chin.

Greaser's knees buckled. He collapsed, face downward, on the floor. Ross, still with his right hand in trousers pocket, stood looking down at him.

Vic Lundy whistled softly a snatch of "Buffalo Gals" without seeming to know that he did it. Then, noting Ross's pocketed hand, "Why didn't you drill him with that derringer?" he asked curiously.

"Derringer?" Ross grunted absently. "What derringer?"

"The one in your pants pocket," Vic said. Then he gaped at Ross; suddenly threw back his head and roared, "You haven't got a derringer! You played one on Keith and me!"

Ross grinned narrowly.

"I knew you had me covered under the

table," he said. "This gladiator one of your outfit?"

"Nary speck!" Vic denied. "Orval, he rode out of Rawles sometimes, but Greaser's a sort of independent fellow. In the horse business, Greaser is, and a right hard-working business man, too. But he goes in for cows too, when there's any money in 'em."

"I'll bet," Ross nodded dryly, watching the unconscious one.

He stooped swiftly and twitched the Colts out of their holsters; stood up and waited until, an instant later, Greaser's shoulders twitched. The lanky figure writhed; Greaser put out a hand and propped himself from the floor.

"Get up!" snapped Ross. "Get up and get out of here! And the next time you want to chew a notch on your gun, pick out a boy about ten years old. A sick Mexican boy would be about your size. You're certainly a weak prop for a pair of hog-legs!"

Shakily Greaser got to his feet. His face wore an expression of bewilderment so ludicrous that Vic and some others of the Rawles men who had gathered about burst into a bellow of laughter. Greaser's face went darker still with angry blood; he glared at Ross.

"Don't yuh figger this settles the cat-hop!" he snarled.

"It'd better settle it!" Ross retorted with cold menace. "Listen, fellow! I have got your record as a sneaking horse-thief. All right! I'm giving you notice right now to get out of Rayo County and stay out. If I catch you inside the county line after today, I'll hang your hide on the fence. Here! Take your guns and hike! If I had a bit of evidence against you, I'd gather you in now. But you mind what I'm telling you, about leaving Rayo County. Git!"

Sullenly Greaser accepted the proffered Colts and reholstered them. Then he whirled and went stalking out. Ross watched him narrowly, alert against any sudden move of the lanky man's. But he heard the click of Greaser's boot-heels receding on the plank veranda.

"So you downed Orval, huh?" Vic Lundy remarked colorlessly. "But Orval had some fellow with him."

"Emory Glass, Wesley Jannett, and a chunky man with a green silk neckerchief," Ross nodded. "They'd lifted a bunch of Flying-X horses and when I rode along, coming here this morning, Orval cracked down on me. I *accidentally* downed Orval and Jannett and Glass."

"And Swede Oll?" inquired a man standing near by, watching Ross very grimly. "Yuh downed him too?"

"No-o. Swede, if that's the fellow with the green bandanna, he said he wasn't in with the others in the rustling. He just took a hand in smoking me up because it was so much fun. I had to drill his shoulder. Then he started back to Rayo along with the horses."

"Good thing yuh never downed Swede!" the man informed him ominously, looking about at the other Rawles citizens around him and seeming to find backing in their faces for his belligerence. "Yes, sir! She certainly is!"

Ross regarded him thoughtfully. He was a hard-faced cowboy in the early twenties, with nothing to set him apart from fifty others, unless it was his unruly shock of sandy hair. Ross rather doubted if, alone, the sandy-haired one would show so much war paint. Nor could he read in the faces of the others any particular heat to match the speaker's.

"Fellow!" he said quietly. "You're talking to the sheriff now. And sheriffs, you ought to know, don't rightfully down a man they can take in. But, if they do down 'em, why, they down 'em — and what have you got to say to that?"

"Well, she's certainly a good thing yuh never got Swede, all the same!" the sandy-haired one repeated somewhat aimlessly, while one or two of his companions grinned with grim amusement.

Ross grinned tolerantly and moved over to the door. He saw, well down the street, the gaunt figure of Greaser, head and shoulder above a group of men. The tall brother of Orval was standing beside a big black horse and something about that animal arrested Ross's curious stare. For a moment he studied it, then turned about — and faced Keith Kawrie, who had come noiselessly up behind him.

"Your stay's becoming a trifle hectic?" Kawrie inquired, with a flicker of amusement in his dark face. "I'm sorry, but being sheriff does entail certain risks."

"Oh, I'm not kicking," Ross grunted with the beginning of a small, grim smile. "You're showing yourself — you Rawles folks — to be real friendly citizens. Now, I'm wondering about something."

"Yes?" Kawrie's eyelids flickered, if his face was blank.

"That fellow, Greaser, that I had to knock out a spell back — I'm afraid he's a horse-thief."

"Do you speak in a general way, or is the allusion specific?"

"Mighty specific!" Ross said grimly. "He's holding a stolen horse right now, if my eyes don't play a trick on me."

"Then, as sheriff, there's nothing to do but gather him in, is there?"

"Nary a thing!" Ross shrugged. "Point is, how much sympathy will Rawles give me if I do start the gathering? Will it be hands off?"

"Hands off!" Keith assured him smilingly, after an instant of hard staring. "But, before you start, I want to say that the two men with Greaser are good friends of his. They're not Rawles citizens, Mr. Sheriff. So what they — ah — may do is not to be charged to us."

"The one there, next to Greaser in height — why, I saw him in Ellard's gang the other night," drawled Ross.

"Koster!" Kawrie nodded, after a glance out the door. His dark eyes were glittering a little and his thin mouth was tight. "I rather wondered about Koster. Go ahead; go as far as you like. The street's yours, Mr. Sheriff!"

Ross stepped through the saloon door and started down the planked veranda toward Greaser Quett and the two men to whom the lanky horse-thief was talking earnestly. He was half way to them when Greaser seemed to catch the hump of his boot-heels and turned a swift head to look. Ross went on, hands swinging freely, so that they brushed gently the checked walnut stocks of his twin Colts as he walked.

The two other men had turned, also; so three faces were toward Ross. He came up and, ignoring all but Greaser, stopped five feet away and glanced at the brand on the rangy black whose reins Greaser held. A hair-branding job it was; a good one but still, knowing what he knew of the Flying-X brand, it was not hard to see the original outline of those letters beneath the crude Cross-in-a-Box into which the Flying-X had been transformed.

Chapter Fourteen

Greaser regarded him with the steady malevolence of a waiting rattler. That the other two men knew him and were equally ready to take swift action in support of the lanky one, Ross realized perfectly. And out of the corner of his eye he kept close watch upon them.

"You didn't hightail it," he remarked in a low voice to Greaser. "Well, I'm sort of glad of it now."

Greaser's eyes narrowed swiftly. He seemed taken aback at this semblance of weakening on the sheriff's part.

"What're you drivin' at?" he snarled uncertainly.

"I said that if I caught you in Rayo County after today I'd shuck that long hide of yours off you just as sure as I'd skin any other side-winder!" Ross informed him in the same even tone. "I told you, too, that you had the name of being a horse-thief and that, if I had any evidence, I'd certainly put you where the little dogs couldn't bite you — right now. Well, I have got that evidence."

He jerked his head toward the black horse, and despite himself Greaser's long, sallow face moved that way also. The two men who stood beside him at the gelding's shapely head almost imperceptibly moved to drift apart — a maneuver which made it difficult for Ross to watch all three. But he turned a trifle and bestowed upon each of them a glance that mirrored complete understanding. They stopped short.

"What the hell yuh talkin' about!" Greaser blustered. "Evidence! What yuh think yuh're pullin', anyhow?"

"Nice job of hair-branding," Ross grinned. "Of course, a fellow that's had all the practice you've had *ought* to do a nice job. Cross-in-a-Box! H'm! I'm thinking that maybe I misjudged you, back in the saloon. Fellow'd think you did have a little smidgin of imagination, after all! Listen!"

Abruptly his voice changed, hardened to cold menace.

"You're under arrest for theft — horse-theft — stealing Flying-X horses. I'm warning you to come along peaceably — Ah! You would!"

He pulled both Colts and shot Greaser through his right forearm twice, turned just a little and unloaded his left-hand gun at this practically point-blank range into the two others, who had gone into action as promptly as had Greaser. Something struck the crown of his hat like a club. Something else burned his left forearm from wrist to elbow and he flinched so that the last two bullets from that pistol went wild.

But when Kieth Kawrie, Vic Lundy and others of the Rawles clan came up to see the result, he was the only one on his feet. One man sprawled uncouthly on his face with outflung arms; Greaser lay groaning, grasping with left hand his broken right arm; the other man was sitting up, wringing his left hand through which a bullet had gone and with great tears rolling down his

149

stubbled cheeks, apparently regardless of the wound in his right shoulder.

Ross was gritting his teeth against the pain of the wound in his own left arm that burned as if a red-hot bar had seared it. But he turned at sound of the footsteps, alert in this savage community for some swift change in the sentiment toward him. Instinctively he began to eject the shells from one Colt and reloaded. Keith Kawrie grinned a little, as if understanding the thought that inspired this action.

"You're a great deal luckier than I ever thought you could be," he said noncommittally, glancing down at the figures on the ground. "Ye-es, much luckier."

"I gathered you didn't allow me much more than the time I took to get down here," Ross nodded. "Well, never mind that now. I'm taking Greaser, here, back to Rayo with me. Koster, I'm afraid, wouldn't be much more than a sort of exhibit — one of those examples of the horrible effects of criminal careers. This other one — life's too short to monkey with every two-by-four hairpin in the county, when so many curly wolves are galloping around. He can hightail it, for all me."

"Good riddance to Koster!" Keith snarled. "He had his nerve with him — coming into *my* town with Ellard's brand on him. If you hadn't downed him, I'd have had the boys dust up the street with him — he being connected to the loop end of a lariat, understood. And this other one, who's doubtless of the Koster stripe —

"Get up from there and stop that howling, you! Get out of Rawles right now, and don't come back, if you don't want to be used up by the street cleaning crew!"

The worthy of the punctured hand took him at his word — and the flame in Keith's full-lidded black eyes was enough to give any thoughtful man material for reflection. Ross, watching him as he finished the loading of his second Colt and jammed it back in its holster, wondered how much of Kawrie's anger was due to the "nerve" of the Ellard man, Koster, and how much to his own victory over Greaser, Koster and this other gunman. For that Keith Kawrie wished him ill, he had no doubt.

"Anybody in camp that can patch Greaser up a little, enough so's I can take him in to the county seat?" he asked. Then suddenly; "You don't mind my taking him to Rayo, do you, Kawrie?"

"Take him to hell, if you want to!" Kawrie snarled. "I don't mind telling you — I don't mind in the least! — that you wouldn't have

151

taken Orval Quett or the others out of Rawles. But since they couldn't hold up their end against one man, what happened is nothing to me. Flint will work on Greaser for you. He's a damn' sight better doctor than moralist."

"I hope so!" Ross shrugged dryly. "Out of some several things I don't really care about in Rayo County, that fellow just about tops the list."

"Perhaps the things you don't like about the county won't bother you so much later on," suggested Kawrie somberly, and Ross had no difficulty in deciding what was meant.

"I'm aiming to fix things so there won't *be* so much to bother me," he countered recklessly, grinning in Kawrie's sullen face. "Let's get Isidor to operating. Long's he's working on this fellow, I won't care how good he is."

Ross ate leathery steak and grease-logged potatoes, and drank thick black coffee at the Mexican hash joint next to the biggest saloon. Then, in company with Vic Lundy, who had become his very shadow, he went back into the saloon, to wait and wonder when the invisible Kawrie would announce himself ready to head for Rayo.

He could see Greaser Quett from where

he sat at a table with Vic. Flint had bandaged the tall man's wounds and he lay on a dirty blanket in a corner of the big, barn-like room. Flint came gliding over to Ross to say in his sanctimonious whine that Greaser would be able to ride later on. Ross shrugged silently, making no secret of his distaste for the frockcoated hypocrite.

Then Ed Nowle came in and looked around, nodding as an old acquaintance to several in the room. He regarded Ross somewhat defiantly and Vic Lundy's little eyes twinkled maliciously as he watched the boy. Ross saw Vic's shoulders shaking as with amusement at some private jest. He wondered what the undercurrent might be, but was too wise to try to pump Vic.

"Not so many of your boys in town, Vic," he remarked suddenly. "They have a business deal on that took some of 'em out of camp?"

"Never can tell," Vic grinned, and again his shoulders quivered. "This here's a mighty sudden sort of place and things do happen sometimes without a fellow having time to figure out what it's all about till afterward. Some pretty work you did here today. Me, I never could work that hand-over-hand draw you use. You shoot as well with one hand as with the other?"

"Just about," Ross replied, understanding that Vic was not telling what he knew of the reason for that departure Ross had noted, of a fourth or fifth of the camp's population. "Just a matter of practicing. They tell me you're the fastest proposition in this neck of the woods, Vic — except, maybe, Keith Kawrie."

"Kawrie? Hell! He's nothing at all with a cutter," Vic said quickly, and Ross grinned inwardly at token of this small vanity and jealousy he had roused; emotions which, childish as they might seem, had more than once in the West lighted fierce flames between rival professionals. "It's Kawrie's head for scheming that keeps him horseback, not his gunplay. I've never yet seen the hairpin could pull quicker than me — or outshoot me, either!"

Ross had an idea. This not-too-bright gunman might prove, all unconsciously, a valuable card in Rawles. The thing to do, right now, was to build friendliness in Vic's mind — friendliness for himself.

"I always figured the cross-arm draw was faster than a straight draw, for using two guns," he said, with just the right shade of uncertainty in his tone. "You say you use the straight draw?"

"Sure! And if the cross-draw's faster —

well, I've never seen it proved to me! Look here!"

He seemed to wriggle where he sat — and it was an awkward posture for getting out his guns. They flashed into sight on a level with the table's edge. The bartender across the room had just straightened up from his whisky barrel under the bar and was turning with a tin cup of liquor in his hand. Vic's right-hand gun roared and the cup leaped from the bartender's hand to go rolling on the bar. The left-hand gun barked in its turn and again the cup rang and leaped.

"My gosh!" Ross breathed, widening his eyes artfully. "Fellow, don't you ever go bothering about cross-arm draws. Anybody that shoots as well as that won't need to have anybody show him new tricks. I was going to show you how to do the cross-arm draw, but now I won't try to show you anything!"

Vic grinned like a pleased child as he replaced the spent shells.

"You see, those fellows you stacked up against earlier — they weren't what I'd call gunsharps, son," he told Ross patronizingly. "Just plain folks, packing a gun and plenty able to get her out and shoot her. But not by any means more than that. You made a right pretty play against 'em and I'm telling you so. Any time a gent goes smoking it with three fellows, he's likely to meet Old Man Trouble face-to-face. No matter if they aren't sharps. And I'm the first man to give you credit for coming out standing up."

"Thanks!" Ross said gravely. "But I don't want you to think I was getting swelled up about my gunplay."

"It's all right!" Vic grinned. "I never thought you was — much. But you took a whole mule-load on to yourself, son, when you pinned on that little nickle-plated star, and I sort of like your style. So I'm telling you this, good-natured like, to keep you out of grief. When you go rambling around this country, you want to remember that there's some right salty customers around. Some of the boys — that fellow Ellard, for one — is almost as good as I am with their guns!"

"Ready to go?" Keith Kawrie inquired, appearing, as he seemed always to, without sound to announce his coming. "Vic, will you get that Cross-in-a-Box black for Greaser to ride?"

"Sure," Vic said slowly, but to Ross's amusement his shrug seemed a trifle sullen. Ross wondered if he had managed to fan a little the jealousy Vic owned for Kawrie.

CHAPTER FIFTEEN

They mounted in front of the saloon. Ross tied Greaser's ankles together by a length of lariat beneath the F-X black's belly. Then he swung up, nodded to Keith and lifted a hand to Vic.

"So long!" he said to the squat gunman, and Vic gave him a friendly smile in farewell.

They went at an easy foxtrot down the single street of Rawles and out upon the Rayo road. Greaser led the little cavalcade; Ross pushed up until his horse was shoulder-to-shoulder with Kawrie's buckskin. He looked at Kawrie smilingly, for he was thinking, just then, of the peculiar grins worn by those of Rawles they had passed on the way out of camp.

"I'd better say one thing right now," he drawled. "There's something in the air — I don't know just what. But if you're figuring any sort of grandstand play — getting yourself rescued from the clutches of the sheriff by your faithful men, or anything like that, you'd better refigure the deal. For it'd certainly be a fatal error — fatal to several folks."

"You're an open-minded sort of young man, aren't you?" Kawrie returned with very obvious amusement. "But doesn't it occur to your innocent mind that if I hadn't wanted to come to Rayo with you today I wouldn't have bothered about so cumbersome a plan as rescue? I'd merely have told you that, however it pained me to refuse, refuse I did."

"And then?" Ross grinned.

"And then?" mimicked Kawrie. "It would have been your move, you know."

"I'm wondering," Ross drawled with leg crooked about the saddle-horn, building a cigarette, "if I can make you believe one thing: that any time I tell you something I mean every word of it? Just for instance: if you'd decided you didn't want to come along peaceably with me today, do you believe that either you'd have come along — or stayed right there in Rawles for the next several hundred years?"

Keith Kawrie grinned mockingly.

"Well, you surely would have!" Ross assured him cheerfully. "Not the whole camp could have got you loose from me, while you were still alive. And so I'm telling you right now that if there's any monkey work planned for between here and Rayo — well, it's certainly at your own risk, Kawrie."

"I've honored you in the past couple of days by a good bit of my thoughts," Kawrie said slowly, sitting sideways and making a cigarette in his turn. "Thinking matters over, it has seemed to me that the — oh, passive indorsement I gave Troop, as sheriff, isn't to be extended to you in that office. Troop realized that he was alone between two fires. So he acted like a wise man and sided with us."

"Something I can't do, of course," Ross answered absently, with eyes upon the little gold thing in Kawrie's fingers, some sort of trick lighter which Kawrie clicked, set against his cigarette-end, then swung on his forefinger by its ring. "As I look at the deal, it's a matter of clearing the county of both your gang of outlaws and Ellards. So far as the law and right of things are concerned, there's nothing to choose between you. So out you both go!"

"Perhaps! I have intended clearing Rayo County of Ellard's outfit, myself."

"And I raise you as much again; I'm clearing the county of both of you, and stringing with neither of you while the rope's swinging! That's a cute trick you've got there; never saw one like it. Flint clicks on steel and lights a piece of hemp — beats matches."

Kawrie looked down as if realizing for the first time what he held in his hand. He shrugged impatiently, as if irritated by the digression.

"Won it from a drummer over at Vado, couple of weeks ago. Well, you've certainly a well-developed bump of confidence! You're just going to clear both outfits out — like that!"

"Oh, there's nothing much to that," Ross grinned pleasantly. "In fact, the hardest job I've got, the one I don't just figure yet, is keeping an eye on Ed Nowle."

That shot went under Keith Kawrie's schooled poise. He made no pretense of not understanding. If ever a man had stared at Ross, with hot murder in his eyes, Keith Kawrie stared now.

"So" — his voice was thick and shaking — "so that's the way the land lies! You've been trespassing on that preserve, have you?"

"Me, I never go rambling through a line fence, if I think the fellow who put it up had a right to do it," Ross said thoughtfully. "But when I don't believe he had a right; when I — Look here, Kawrie, do you think for a minute you're fit to even walk down the same side of the street with any decent woman? Take a look at yourself, man! You're some sort of scalawag kicked out of your home town. Likely there's a warrant — or two or three — out for you, back there. Now do you figure for a minute that I'm going to stand by peaceably and watch you pull your dirty schemes here?"

He had begun in a light, even tone, but by the time he had spat out his last words, he was leaning toward Keith Kawrie with all masks dropped, glaring at the gang leader as viciously as Kawrie in his turn glared at him.

"And don't think I don't see your play with Ed!" Ross said grimly. "You want to get him tangled up so you can hold that over her head, don't you? I haven't figured how I'll do it, but I promise you I'll put a spike in that too."

Then they rode on, watching each other, until before them on the trail loomed the deserted cabin where Ross had left Pat Phelan with Swede Oll and the Flying-X horses. Ross's eyes were roving, so he saw the emptiness of the corral behind the cabin, caught the indefinable atmosphere of desertion about the cabin itself, and at the same moment observed Kawrie's tiny smile of triumph.

"Come on!" he snapped at Kawrie. "Give that goat of yours the leather and let's see what's happening."

"Has happened," corrected Kawrie. "I deduce from your transparent expression

161

that you left someone — your deputy? — here with Oll and the horses?"

"Less talk!" Ross gritted. "If you make me get ugly with you —"

They jumped the animals into a gallop, overtaking Greaser, and Ross swung his quirt viciously upon the rump of the prisoner's black. So the three of them came racing down upon the cabin with the animals nose and nose.

"Pat!" Ross cried. "Pat, old-timer!"

There was a strange choking sound from inside, ending in a groan. Silence for an instant, then a dragging, shuffling noise. Ross's twin Colts leaped into his hands like live things and he crouched a little in the saddle, gaping at the door, but alert to see from the tail of his eyes any move of Kawrie or Greaser.

Then in the doorway appeared Pat Phelan, crawling weakly. He clawed at the door jamb and pulled himself erect. His red hair was matted with blood, his square, pugnacious face had more the semblance of raw beef than a human countenance; his left arm hung with a tell-tale limpness and one of his ears was almost severed from his head. But holding himself erect there by the door facing, he essayed a grin through swollen lips.

"Sure and you might be calling me one hell of deputy!" he croaked. "I was taken unsuspicioning and nine-ten of the devils beat me over the head and never a one of them did I collect, myself. That scoundrel you left here, *he* hightailed with the others and, I'm thinking, the horses. I was but getting my senses when you called."

Ross swung down and, managing to keep his guns ready, inspected his lieutenant. So far as he could see, Pat's damages were but superficial. He would be a sore Irishman for a week or two, but Ross was thankful that the gang had not been so bloodthirsty as to kill the deputy.

Sympathize with Pat as he might, there was still the matter of the rescue to be considered, and decision to be made about counteracting it. That it had been effected by those men of Rawles, and so of Keith Kawrie's, who had galloped out of the little camp that afternoon, to come down this Rayo road and stumble upon the Flying-X horses in the corral here, he had no doubt. All the grins of the men upon the street in Rawles had been because they had expected this dénouement. Keith Kawrie's secret amusement — which had been not too secret — was also born of this same coup upon the Sheriff of Rayo County.

Slowly, whistling softly between his teeth, Ross turned to the kingpin of the Rawles riders and to the sullen, wounded horse-thief, Greaser Quett, who had not spoken a word since their departure from Rawles.

"Better get down, you-all," he told them expressionlessly. "Got to look around and wawa a little about this business."

He cut the bonds on Greaser's feet. Without remark, they swung off and trailed their horses' bridle reins. Ross decided that neither considered active hostility just then. Indeed, Keith Kawrie seemed to be greatly interested and amused in studying Pat. Greaser, after one flash of malicious pleasure, slouched over to the shadow of the cabin wall and sprawled at length there, indifferent to what befell.

With a spare shirt from his saddle-bags, Ross bandaged Pat's torn ear and set the broken left forearm between two small sticks. Pat waved him off at this, declaring impatiently that his hurts were of no importance.

"Sure, I've still my gun-arm and I never was any use with more'n one hog-leg. The thing that'll cure me quite is seeing those sons over my front sight! What do we be waiting for?"

Ross grinned mirthlessly and looked

164

sidelong at Kawrie.

"Why, I was just wondering, Pat, old-timer. Yes, just wondering. This hot weather, it's just about the devil and all of a lot of trouble to be chasing sticky ropers up and down. Just think how much nicer it is to have 'em change their minds and bring those Flying-X horses back themselves."

"They'll be doing that, of course!" Pat sniffed impatiently..

"Why not?" Ross inquired blandly. "Oh, Kawrie, do you mind sending word to your gang — the ones that took the horses out of the corral, here — to haze 'em all back to the Flying-X? I'd certainly take it kindly if you would!"

"Why, Your Honor!" Kawrie cried mockingly. "What would give you the impression that it was my men who took the horses? I'm surprised — pained, too! — at your attitude. But you're only joking, of course."

"Of course, just joking," Ross nodded, lip-corners lifting slightly. "There's another little slant to the joke. I'm really funny when I do get started, you see: It'd be a fine joke, if Judge Xavier would find his horses back in the pasture almost as soon as he'd discovered he'd lost 'em. But, if he can't do that, I'll have to try to take his mind off the disappointment somehow. And you and I

165

riding into Rayo will likely give him a laugh — the way we'll ride."

"What do you mean?" Kawrie's hands had crept up until they were at his waist. "Just what do you mean?"

"Why" — Ross surveyed him with eyes narrowed, like one who pictures inwardly an amusing scene — "first you'll come riding allasame warwhoop: naked, you know, except for a little bandanna breeching. You'll be all painted up, with turkey feathers in your hair. And — and — you'll have a sign hanging down your front: 'The Curly Wolf of Rawles'!"

For all his seeming preoccupation with this delightful picture, he was watching the trembling hands of Keith Kawrie and at just the proper moment, "Pull 'em any time you're minded to, Kawrie," he drawled. "I'll see if I can't promote Vic a little."

Kawrie's hands were hooked like claws; they clenched, unclenched, but somehow went no nearer the butts of his Colts. Perhaps he was recalling the scene on the Rawles street that morning, when Ross had gone into flashing action against three and had been the only one remaining on his feet when the smoke wreaths drifted away.

"You — you wouldn't dare!" he said thickly. "You — I — we'd stake you out on an ant-hill minus your hide. We —"

"Shucks!" Ross cried genially. "You're talking through your Stetson and you know it! Vic'd kill himself laughing. You'd never dare show your face in the country again. Old Mexico'd be the only place you could live. 'Keith Warwhoop,' they'd name you. Or 'Big Chief Feather Duster.' The very kids would hurrah the life out of you."

He shrugged genially.

"Of course, it doesn't have to come off, you know. Tell you what, Kawrie: if those horses get back into the Flying-X pasture right away, we'll go on into town just as we started. I'll let you arrange for bail and say nothing about this business. What do you say? Horse — or — feathers?"

"Who could go?" Kawrie demanded sullenly.

"Ed," Ross said, who had just turned his head swiftly toward the trail, where the pound of a loping horse's hoofs sounded faintly. "He's coming. Just tell him where to find the men and the horses."

Kawrie lifted a shoulder in a sulky gesture, then waved to the slender, oncoming rider. Ed spurred up the slope off the trail and reined in to stare curiously at the group.

"Ed," Keith Kawrie said evenly, "go to Knife Parra and say that I want those

Flying-X horses, every one of them, put back in Xavier's pasture where Orval Quett got them. Tell him —"

"Tell him where to find your man," Ross interrupted grimly. "Don't be taking so much knowledge for granted, Kawrie. Ed's pretty near a perfect stranger, you know; tell him this is the Rayo road below here."

Kawrie eyed Ross with a malevolence that betrayed perfect understanding of the play. He was not to be permitted to treat Ed Nowle, in the sheriff's presence, as one of his gang, possessed of full information regarding its whereabouts, its activities.

"They'll be coming into Rawles from the mountain road," he explained with a sneer. "Knife Parra is a short, thick-set Mexican with a scar notching his nose."

Ed stared blankly. Evidently this play was puzzling him. This Ross saw. So he stepped in.

"Speed's the essence of that contract, Ed," Ross drawled. "We'll be going on into Rayo."

Ed nodded, still a little dazed of expression. Ross turned to his prisoners.

"Let's go! Greaser! Come on; get aboard. Next stop's the county seat!"

They saw Ed vanish over a ridge, then pushed on rapidly toward Rayo. Kawrie let his buckskin lag a little, until Ross caught up with him. Then, staring narrow-eyed at his cheerful captor, he growled, "I said a while ago that you wouldn't have our endorsement. Now, I'll tell you something else: very soon, I'm going to kill you."

"Goodness!" Ross grinned. "Is that all that's worrying you? Hop to it, Big Chief! Hop to it!"

CHAPTER SIXTEEN

On the edge of Rayo, Keith Kawrie drew up abruptly and faced Ross.

"I'm figuring you as an enemy, Varney. Make no mistake about that. But even between enemies certain formalities can be observed. You made a bargain back yonder; you said that —"

"That if you had those Flying-X horses back in the pasture by the time we hit Rayo, I'd go ahead, as I promised in Rawles, and let you arrange for bail," Ross interrupted him with a slight, contemptuous grin. "Listen, Kawrie, there's not a thing wrong with my memory — or with my word; either! I'm going to do even more than I promised, in order to do what I promised."

"What do you mean by that?" Kawrie frowned suspiciously.

"I mean, if I told Judge Xavier that you were the gentleman who had his stuff rustled, you'd have a sweet time getting bail on the stick-up charge, now wouldn't you? He'd not only refuse you bail, he'd swear out a warrant on the horse-stealing charge!"

"I haven't admitted that I had anything whatever to do with stealing his horses. Merely because I have a certain authority and can arrange to have the thieves —"

"Ah, shut up!" Ross cried; and certain citizens of the county seat, who had been staring curiously, if not demonstratively, at this quartet of horsemen, lifted their eyebrows amazedly. "Are you trying to play peekaboo with me? False faces do fool kids, Kawrie, but you might as well forget that brand of talk when we're ready to make bail. You'll have to do it from the jail, though. Hereafter, every prisoner I bring in is going to a cell until he's let out according to law."

"But —" Kawrie began angrily.

"Shut up!" Ross snapped again, and brought his quirt-lash down on Kawrie's horse. "From now until you make bond, I'm running the show. I'll do everything I promised you, but I'll do it my own way."

He had not seen anyone moving ahead of them, from the ranks of the townsmen on the sidewalks who watched. But in front of the Swan was gathered a sizable group, and in its van stood Lake Ellard with marshal's star prominent on his coat front. Beside him, each with his hands upon the butts of his twin Colts, stood that slender, yellow-eyed killer in vivid red shirt, known as "Buckshot," and a fattish, red-faced, fiercely scowling one-eyed man.

"Well!" Ross cried. "Looks like a reception committee."

"Ellard, Buckshot and Talbot," Kawrie said grimly. "It looks to me, Varney, as if you had bitten off rather more than you can chew! There are forty men behind Ellard and his deputies. I'd gladly try conclusions with Ellard alone, but —"

"But you're a prisoner — my prisoner — right now," Ross said evenly. "So, unless I give you the word to start smoking it, you'll keep your gun holstered. Not Ellard nor anybody else is going to touch a prisoner of mine!"

"Howdy!" Ellard said, as perforce the cavalcade drew rein before the group standing in the center of the street. "So you *did* get him. Well, I'll take him off your hands."

"You'll take *which* him off my hands?" Ross inquired, staring with puzzled face down into the cold gray eyes.

"Kawrie. I got several charges against him."

"Sorry," Ross answered. "But right now he's got an urgent appointment to keep, up at the jail. When that's settled, either he'll stay in one of the cells or go out on bond. If he stays to board in my hotel a while, of course he'll just stay. But if he's let out on bond and you want him, you can surely have him. But you'll have to do your own catching, of course."

"I said," Ellard breathed in the deadly whisper Ross had heard him use once before, and with pale face like gray stone, "I'll take him off your hands — now."

"Kawrie," Ross said quietly, "don't pull those guns. Not until I've pulled mine. Then you have the right to protect yourself that any man's got when he's up against an illegal attack on his life. Ellard! You can't have Kawrie. The only way you can take him is by downing my deputy and me. And I promise you one thing — I'm damned if *I* would think of being downed before I got you! Now, get out of the road and let me go on with my prisoners — or else start your wolf howling. We'll join in the chorus!"

Pat Phelan, with the pale and shaky Greaser at his stirrup, came pushing up to join Ross and Kawrie in making a solid front in the marshal's face.

"Sure, and she's a fine large day!" Pat said with a dancing devil in his small blue eyes. "Look up, all of you! For many of you'll never see another — it may be. So look long at this one."

Still meeting Ellard's chill, light eyes, Ross sat with folded arms and whistled through his teeth — whistled "The Dying Ranger." It was a hard situation for Lake Ellard, and Ross was careful to do nothing to make it easier. Ellard must have known that, standing there as he did, he was an excellent target for a bullet from one of these three; that his first hostile move would fill that dusty street with the smoke of homeric battle. Yet no flicker of emotion showed on his hard face.

"What seems to be the — ah — difficulty?" inquired a precise, quite audible voice from the roof of the Swan.

Automatically, every eye shuttled to the frock-coated and portly figure of Judge Xavier, who stood with a foot comfortably upon the 'dobe parapet of the street wall, hat pushed back and one bright black eye squinted against the smoke of his thin cheroot. Around the judge were a half-dozen citizens. Each, like the judge, carried handily either rifle or double-barreled shotgun.

"Just a little argument about jurisdiction," Ross grinned. "Ellard, he's kind of got into a bad habit of running everything around here and aimed to annex the sheriff's office this nice evening. I am just about to show him the error of his judgment."

"Tchk! Tchk!" said the judge sadly. "It seems to me that the duties and so the jurisdictions of the two offices should be so plain as to make mistakes impossible. But, sitting — or leaning — more or less informally, may I, as District Judge, be permitted to assist in the difficulties? Thanks! I am taking unanimous consent for granted, being in a sense a higher court. Just what is the specific point involved, Mr. Sheriff?"

"Why, I brought in Kawrie, here, to answer a charge of highway robbery," Ross said. "Now Ellard says that he's the proper custodian of the prisoner. *My* idea is that, if the honorable city marshal had really pined for Kawrie he should have collected him the other night when Kawrie rode down the street so gaily and so free."

"Why, there's no argument possible there!" cried Judge Xavier genially. "I'm surprised that one arose. Mr. Ellard has been misinformed, or ill-advised. I recall the nature of the charge against Mr. Kaw-rie, and the alleged offense is said to have taken place outside the limits of Rayo. Therefore, the sheriff is paramount. Even if this were not the case, no city marshal has any shadow of legal authority to justify an attempt to — ah — remove a prisoner from shrieval custody."

"In other words," Ellard snarled, "you're siding nowadays with the sheriff! Is that it, Judge?"

"I question the term 'nowadays,' " the judge said calmly. "To one of legal mind, it is too general and too irrevocable. But in the present instance I most assuredly do side with the sheriff's office. One could not do otherwise, legally. So, Mr. Ellard, you will please clear the street and let the sheriff proceed with his prisoners."

"This," Ellard said in his low, deadly voice, "is one time you got the downhill drag on me. But I'm figuring it's going to be the last time, young fellow!"

With which he whirled and moved toward the Swan's door. After a moment of hesitation, Talbot and the yellow-eyed Buckshot followed him. The crowd opened up silently to let Ross and his companions go on up the street toward the jail.

"Well," Ross grinned, "I certainly feel as if

somebody had handed me the other half of my life — and you can write in 'Judge Xavier' for 'somebody.' "

"You think that ends it?" scoffed Keith Kawrie somberly. "Like hell it does! You've got me into a fine mess! Ellard will go to that little cur, District Attorney Irlan. Irlan will object to my bond and so I'll be here, stuck!"

"There's one thing you're rather overlooking," Ross told him with a humorless smile. "That's the fact that I happen to be sheriff of this county, and when I get a warrant to serve, I'll serve it or get overpowered by the smoke. Whether or not the fellow a sheriff's after can arrange bond, or whether or not the officials here like that fellow, that doesn't bother me a bit. I'd have got you one way or another in Rawles, Kawrie, and you can lay the last dollar you'll ever steal on that. Not that you don't know it!"

At the jail a lengthy man uncoiled himself from a chair in Ross's office. He grinned in saturnine fashion at Keith Kawrie.

"I've been waiting for quite a spell," he drawled. "When I saw what was going on down by the Swan, I couldn't rightly make out whether I was going to bond you out, Keith, or make arrangements for burying you."

He turned to Ross.

"Mr. Sheriff, my name's Young, Briley Young. I'm a cattle-buyer and I'm ready to bail out Kawrie right now — cash bond, too."

"Young, Young," Ross repeated thoughtfully. "I don't seem to recall the name, but I've heard about you — I reckon you're the only cattle-buyer to find a lot of business in Rawles."

"Maybe," Young shrugged calmly. "But right now it's the bond business that's on my mind. How much will it be? Thousand?"

"Now, now," Ross checked him gently, grinning a little. "That's the old way of doing it. Nowadays it's a lot more refined, and complicated. Whenever the District Court meets, I take Kawrie in. The judge listens to the arguments and decides to grant bond or not to grant it. I'm nothing but the faithful servant of the law, Mr. — Young, you said, didn't you?"

Judge Xavier came into the office, and the deceptively good-humored smile which he had worn while standing upon the Swan's roof was no longer in evidence. Now his black eyes were hard, his broad, smooth-shaven face indubitably peevish.

"Kawrie!" he cried angrily. "You're undoubtedly stick-fingered! I've kept a sort of judicial aloofness in this quarrel between your clan and Lake Ellard's; I've tried to steer a legal and common-sensible course between the rocks that have been chunked in your war. But when you — or your merry men, it's all the same — come raiding my property and running off my valuable horses, then certainly you are putting a heavy tax on my forbearance!"

"Just a minute, Judge," Ross broke in with a small grin. "I found your horses up on the Rawles trail, early this morning. While I was — well, sort of arguing with the fellows who had 'em about the illegality of their methods, I accidentally downed three of 'em. Orval Quett, Emory Glass and Wesley Jannett, those three were. And I bored a little hole in Swede Oll. Swede got away. He took the hole with him for a souvenir. Then, over in Rawles, Greaser Quett painted up for war on account of his brother Orval, and when I saw the neat and lovely job of hair-branding he'd done on a Flying-X horse, I fetched him in."

"But the horses?" Judge Xavier inquired, strictly unjudicial pleasure beginning to lighten his irritated face.

"Oh, I had 'em sent back to your place. Maybe that wasn't according to Hoyle; it might've been better to bring 'em in here and return 'em to you by process of law or something, but I was pretty busy about then, so I figured that what you'd chiefly want was the horses."

A wizened cowboy clumped hurriedly through the door and looked swiftly around.

"Say, Judge!" he cried. "Them horses, the damn' critters done come back. I don't know how, but they're back an' Curt Prentiss, he says I better ride in an' tell you."

"Thanks!" nodded the judge. "I rather expected that word. Tell Curt that the sheriff found them in possession of Orval Quett, Wesley Jannett and Emory Glass, late citizens of Rawles in this county. Swede Oll and Greaser Quett are alleged to have had a certain connection with the theft and each has undergone an operation. Greaser is recuperating in our interested care, but Mr. Oll's whereabouts are at present unknown."

"Y-yes, sir!" stuttered the wizened cowboy, and went dazedly out. "I'll tell him. Uh — anyhow, I'll *try!*"

"Now, then, about Kawrie, here," Ross remarked thoughtfully. "Without going into details, Judge, he's all ready to show in court and ask for bail."

"Are there any reasons in the sheriff's possession for objecting?"

"Nary one. Ellard, now, he'll likely object

one or two, but not this office."

"I see," the judge nodded, black eyes twinkling. "I was chiefly interested in possible objections of the sheriff. As for the others — well, produce him in court after you eat supper, Mr. Sheriff, with a responsible bondsman or bondsmen."

Chapter Seventeen

"Seems to me, Kawrie," Ross drawled when the judge's portly figure had vanished, "that the best thing you can do is keep sort of close to the office here until court opens. I'm going out and wander a bit, and before I go I'll just collect those Colts of yours and keep 'em while you're in my custody."

"And suppose one of Ellard's glory-hunters jumps me?" Kawrie objected.

"They won't jump you while you stay here!" Ross assured him with much grimness. "And either you stay right here in the office or I lock you up until you've made bond."

Kawrie lifted a shoulder in unwilling affirmation. He pulled the Colts from his holsters. Ross took them and dropped them into the drawer of the table. Kawrie's eyes followed the maneuver intently.

"Come on, Pat," Ross said to his deputy.

"And whither away?" Pat inquired as Ross, instead of going along the main street in the direction of the Swan, turned toward the adobe houses that, scattered seemingly at random in the rear of the main thoroughfare, housed a good many of the town's prominent citizens.

"Notice that fellow Young, as he calls himself?" Ross grunted, without heeding Pat's query. "Remember him?"

"Ummm!" Pat screwed up his eyes thoughtfully. "Don't seem to. . . . Yeh! Sure, he was in Del Rio the night we fell foul of the two killers from Lincoln County. And then again that day in Alamito! But did you get his name that time in Del Rio? The name he was using then?"

"Uh-uh. Don't know that it matters anyhow. But he's from our part of the country, old-timer; and he's thick with Kawrie and that Rawles gang. I'm thinking that maybe, just maybe, he knows quite a little about the story of Tecolote sticking up that stage."

"Can happen!" Pat cried. "Well?"

They had come to a long adobe house set well back behind a neatly whitewashed picket fence; a well-kept house with long adobe-pillared front gallery bordered by bright flowers. At the gate Ross stopped short; his heart was pounding a little with sight of a slender, blue-ginghamed figure sitting in the gallery with a pan upon her lap.

"You skip around town and see what you can pick up about the horrible details of that stage robbery, Pat," he said, with eyes lifted over the deputy's head to study intently the twilight sky. "I — I'll catch up with you."

"Huh?" Pat said, staring hard.

Then he looked at the gallery, and his eyes narrowed; a small twitching attacked the corners of his wide, thin mouth.

"Oh!" he grunted expressively. "All right."

He went rolling on, with his right thumb hooked in his crossed cartridge belt, head thrown back, singing very clearly as he went:

"Sure, I done fell in love again;
Never thought I'd do it!
But I really never had a chance —
Slipped before I knew it!"

Ross lifted the bale of the gate and went inside. Very deliberately and painstakingly indeed did he see to the gate's closing. For he knew that a pair of calm brown eyes were observing him, and half he was dreading the talk with Marie Nowle, while half he would have waded through the combined arrays of Lake Ellard and Keith Kawrie to get to talk to her. He dropped the bale over a picket and went clicking up the graveled walk, brown face blank, humming the snatch of melody Pat was singing.

"Evening," he greeted her gravely. She nodded silently. "Mind if I sit down a few minutes? Thanks."

He propped himself against one of the big pillars almost at her feet and very thoughtfully regarded the clear oval of her face.

"Wouldn't there be hell afloat and the river rising," he wondered, "if I should say to her 'I'm that awful El Tecolote you've heard about! Yes, me! Plain Ross Varney from the south.' "

"So El Tecolote did come!" she remarked abruptly, and at this seeming mind-reading he looked startled. "Why, what's the matter?"

"I was just wondering about that." He shrugged. "Wondering if — if he really had showed up in Rayo County to stick up the stage."

"Why should you doubt it?" She frowned. "Plenty of other outlaws have been attracted here; why not El Tecolote?"

"I was thinking that maybe it was like the case of other outlaws — a home-raised boy pulls a robbery or murder and starts the word that some well-known man or gang did the job."

"But he was recognized; he —"

"You figure Briley Young's reliable?" he interrupted at a venture.

"What reason would he have for bringing such a story into Rayo if it weren't true?"

"Oh, that's a different breed of horse entirely." He grinned.

So it was Young who had started the story. Ross made a resolution to have a long and serious conversation with the imaginative Mr. Young; at the very earliest moment too.

"Not being overly acquainted with him, I can't say what reason he'd have. He might not have any at all — and he might have fifty, every one better than the last."

"How does your job look to you today?" she asked with eyes lowered. "Do you feel that it's impossible to clean up the county?"

"Don't know." Ross shrugged, and at his somber tone she looked up quickly, to find that his face and eyes were gloomier, even, than his voice. "I wasn't worrying about that part particularly. I was wondering if my cleaning it up, in the way it'll naturally have to be cleaned, will make any difference in a — a sort of crazy hope I've been nursing since the other day."

"What —" she began, then suddenly

dropped her eyes, while a slow wave of crimson colored smooth round neck and face. "I mean — what do you mean? But perhaps it's too personal to discuss!" she hurried on.

"I'm afraid you know what I mean," he told her hopelessly. "Funny business. . . . Fellow can go riding heart whole and fancy free for years, spinning his loop as suits him, turning down this trail and that without anything in particular bobbing up to make him want to stop or turn aside or come back, and then, all of a sudden —"

"Mrs. Upson is waiting!" Marie Nowle cried abruptly. She made as if to rise.

"Sit down!" Ross said quietly, flinging up a restraining arm. "The way things go around Rayo County, you're maybe talking and listening to a man that's as good as lying in Boot Hill right now, with a wooden headboard wrapped around his neck. No telling when I'll see you again, especially with a chance to talk to you alone."

He looked steadily at her.

"I was saying, a fellow like that — like me — comes all of a sudden up to a girl who's sitting beside the trail and all bets are off! Nothing behind him makes a bit of difference in the world. For this girl'll begin asking him who he is and — this is worse —

and what he was.

"Take you and me, for example. I reckon I'm a sort of sudden soul. Looking back, it seems to me that most of the things I've done, good, bad and indifferent, come from that habit of mine. And now — Well, for all you know, I'm just a worthless cowpuncher from down south somewhere, or even a rustler or a hold-up man. I'm sheriff of the county; I've killed three men in operating as a peace officer and, if I go on and I'm not downed myself, I'll certainly have to drop a few more in Boot Hill — Lake Ellard and his two deputies, Keith Kawrie and, very likely, Vic Lundy."

"Kawrie!" she cried, staring fixedly at him with a fear in her widened eyes that brought deepest rage to Ross — malignant hatred of the tall, good-looking outlaw leader who sat now in his office at the jail. "I — you —"

"I said Kawrie," he told her grimly. "He furnishes the brains for that Rawles outfit; Vic Lundy supplies the nerve and the gunplay — not that Kawrie's afraid. I don't believe that for a minute. But he's not cut out to kill with the handiness and speed of Vic Lundy.

"But what I'm driving at is, by the time I do the job I contracted with your uncle to do, I'll have a tolerable private plot in Boot

Hill, full of such as the ones I mentioned. Now, when I finish up, if I'm still on my feet, what would a girl say to me, even if she knew I'd done work that had to be done? What would you say to me? I'm telling you now that, the minute I saw you, I — I knew that there was just one girl in all this wide, round world for Ross Varney!"

"I — oh, why do you have to say that!" she whispered, and half of it seemed that she spoke to herself, not to him. Then swiftly she raised her eyes and regarded him levelly. "I don't know what will happen between now and — and that day you speak of. I don't know what I'll think — believe — on that day. How can I? For — for there's more to all this situation here than — than you dream of, Ross Varney."

"Wait a minute!" he said quickly, coming to his feet, with a tigerish straightening of long body, as she got up. "Maybe I understand a good deal more about this situation than you think. So I understand you — understand what you're hinting at, when you say lots of things might happen. But what I was wondering about was just the general part — what you'd think of the killer who had plenty of notches on his guns; but was still a peace officer, a killer only of men who had to be killed."

"I — oh, I don't know. I don't like the thought of that. But — one thing I feel: if a woman, any woman, really loved a man, she'd love him in spite of characteristics, past deeds that she didn't like. If she had thought she loved him, but found that those made a difference, then it would be plain that she couldn't have loved him at all. That sounds like a tangled theory, but it's a fact. Now, I have to go! I don't want to talk any more."

"Nothing else you want to tell me? Nothing about Kawrie? No? Well, where's this cousin of yours, Ed? Has he come back to the N-Bar? To town?"

"I haven't seen him since — since the night he quarreled with his father in the sheriff's office. I'm so afraid — I —"

"What Ed needs," Ross said dispassionately, "is a good, swift kick where it'll hurt most. I recall how, that day I first saw you on the trail, you were on the look-out for him — afraid he'd been mixed up in a stage robbery down that way."

"I was doing no such thing!" she cried, her tone mirroring perfect indignation, but with face showing paper-white by contrast with the soft blue of her apron. "I don't know what you're trying to learn, Mr. Varney, but I assure you that bluffs will get nothing for you!"

"Saw a fellow scallyhooting across the landscape just today," Ross remarked in absent voice. "Could've been Ed. In fact —"

"What do you mean?" she demanded, and this time she could not control her voice. "What was Ed doing?"

"*I* never said he was doing anything. But, you see! You were scared to death then that I had seen him doing something that he oughtn't to have been. Same as on the day I mentioned; the first time I saw you. Marie, can't you come out into the open with me? Don't you know that — I'd just about do anything in the world for you?"

Violently, as if struggling both against her own impulse and his suggestion, she shook her head, scarlet underlip caught between her teeth.

"No! No!" she said gaspingly. "I can't tell you anything. I — I don't know anything. I —"

Then she whirled and rushed into the house, and Ross, after a moment of grim staring after her, turned and walked down the graveled path. He did not go downtown after Pat. Instead, he went to a Chinese restaurant and ate supper, then sent a boy with a meal to Keith Kawrie. Behind a corral he sat smoking for an hour, able to see the door of the sheriff's office without moving. Then he got up and went over to the jail.

"Come on, Kawrie," he said tonelessly. "Down to court with you."

He reached past Kawrie, who sat at the table over the remnants of his meal, and drew the outlaw's Colts from the drawer. He shook his head as Kawrie extended his hands for the weapons.

"I'll tote 'em for you. I don't look for any trouble on the road, but if any begins, between this and the courtroom, I'll give 'em to you and you can start fogging with my word. I'll just jam 'em into the waistband of my trousers. We'll ride down there."

They got their horses from the corral behind the jail. Ross was silent, grim of face. Kawrie watched him closely, somewhat curiously.

"Down the main street," he grunted as they came around the jail to the front. Ross nodded.

"One of these days, pretty soon now, I figure, I'm going to do one of three things," Ross said slowly. "I'm going to kill you, or run you out of the country, or hang you to a cottonwood. But I will say, for all that, I give you credit for having a full-sized supply of nerve. Yes, down the main street."

"As a matter of fact," Kawrie smiled, but without any humor whatever, "you're not destined to do any of the three things you so lightly discuss, I think. I have never planned on becoming a permanent resident of Rayo County; but when I leave, it will be of my own accord and with all my plans fulfilled."

"Now that El Tecolote's here, I reckon you're sort of talking through your hat," Ross shrugged, and Kawrie's grin widened a little.

"I don't think El Tecolote is much to be feared by me," he answered.

"Like hell he's not!" Ross assured him savagely. "If I were you, I'd spend a good deal of time thinking about him! Now, come on and shut up!"

They came, the horses walking, down the main street toward the Swan. No sign of active hostility could Ross detect in the men standing on the veranda. On past it, with Ross watching the street ahead and Keith Kawrie, with a devil-may-care expression on his dark face, seeming to see everything, everywhere about them. Then, out of a saloon not a hundred feet from the courthouse, came the yellow-eyed young deputy marshal, Buckshot, the merest trifle unsteady in his gait. He lurched off the plank-walk and came out in their path.

"What do *you* want?" Ross inquired evenly.

"You think you're hell on wheels, now don't you?" the deputy said unpleasantly. "Just because you had the breaks and the devil's own luck ever since you hit this camp, you think you're something! Well, Lake Ellard's too damn' easy-going with you. Me, I'm going to show you a few. I'm going to clean your plow proper and when I get done —"

He had moved his hands until they rested lightly on the white butts of his Colts. His yellow eyes were flaming, partly with whisky, Ross thought, but partly with a killing lust that obviously he had been nursing for long. The advantage in gunplay was with him, the dismounted man. Ross made no move to draw a weapon. Instead, he cleared his foot of the right stirrup and, with continuation of the flashing movement, kicked Buckshot in the chin.

As the slender, red-shirted figure reeled backward, Ross laid hand upon saddle-horn, lifted himself to fling left leg over the horse's back, then came crashing down upon the deputy with both feet in his face. He kicked a gun out of Buckshot's hand, stooped to jerk the other Colt from its holster and fling it over a house. Buckshot was senseless from that terrific impact and Ross lifted him and hung him over his horse's withers. Then he looked swiftly around.

The men in front of the Swan had crowded a little closer to that end of the saloon veranda which was nearest the courthouse and, so, this present activity. But none moved toward the sheriff. There came a shrill wolf howl. Ross saw Pat Phelan waving a hand from a veranda directly across from the Swan. He smiled grimly at this. Trust Pat to be on hand when needed — and in just the proper position. He turned back to Kawrie.

"Go on into the courthouse and wait there for me. I'll be back in a couple minutes — I reckon."

Kawrie nodded silently. Ross swung up and held the limp Buckshot with one hand, while he kneed the black around and headed him, without touching the bridle reins, back toward the Swan. Coming up to the veranda, he sat staring at the men there, a big, efficient-looking, extremely ill-humored mass. Then, as if the burden were nothing, he lifted Buckshot by a shoulder and a leg, lifted him three feet, then hurled him into the press on the Swan's veranda.

"There's your loud-yapping deputy marshal!" he snarled. "But the next one of you that comes hunting trouble with me, he's certainly going to find it — in the neck. Any more candidates? Thought not. You're a bunch of sneaking coyotes; you have got to have half-man like Lake Ellard or that mouthy kid there, to lead you into anything. I'm sitting right here in front of you and I haven't even pulled a gun. But there's not one of you with guts enough to try to beat me to the draw. Because you know I'd get a half-dozen of you and not one of you has got the cold nerve to take a chance."

He was watching narrowly for the appearance of Ellard. He had no illusions about the marshal. Ellard, doubtless, would be perfectly willing to shoot from the press of silent men there. Nor would it particularly hurt his prestige in that crowd. But once more Ellard was elsewhere. Ross waited a minute, then wheeled his horse and rode at a walk back toward the courthouse. Not a sound could be heard behind him from the Ellard clan.

CHAPTER EIGHTEEN

Ross sat impatiently in the sheriff's office. It was early — he had just eaten and come back, to wait until Pat Phelan brought in Mr. Norman Curtis. While he waited for Mr. Curtis, who had been a passenger on the stage the day El Tecolote was said to have stopped that vehicle on the Vado-Rayo road, Ross's thoughts went grimly to that other passenger of the day of the robbery, Mr. Briley Young, the cattle-buyer and un-official bondsman for the progressive village of Rawles.

Ross had firmly intended that Young should not get out of Rayo until he had explained his reason for bringing to Rayo the word that El Tecolote had been the stage robber. He had keenly wished to learn from Young where he had known El Tecolote in the past and by what means he had recog-nized El Tecolote during the robbery.

But when he had rejoined Keith Kawrie in Judge Xavier's courtroom, the night before, Ross had seen Kawrie admitted to bond with no objections from anyone. He had curtly warned Kawrie to get out of town and stay out, and had watched the outlaw chief mount outside the courthouse and go jogging out to northward, toward

Rawles. Then, held in talk for a time by Judge Xavier after adjournment of the brief session, he had come back looking for Young. But the cattle-buyer had vanished. None seemed to have seen him leave the county seat, but the search of Ross and Pat over the town had not discovered the lanky, blank-faced capitalist.

Thought of Young and Keith Kawrie inevitably brought thought of Marie Nowle. What, Ross wondered, was worrying the girl? Ed, of course, but it seemed to Ross that he sensed a deeper worry than mere cousinly interest justified. For himself, the man in love, he knew that everything else was secondary to his feeling for Marie. Then, he thought, angrily reversing this process, she could not care for him, else Ed and all other things and persons in the world would be secondary to her feeling for him.

Could she be in love with Keith Kawrie? Women did not think as men thought, he told himself bitterly. A big, dark, handsome man — one, too, of education and polish — might well turn a girl's head in this lonely community, where her other associates were, in the main, rough diamonds. He had no egotism concerning his own personality. He considered himself merely a big ordinary sort of cowpuncher, by the accident of circumstance veneered with three semesters of what might be termed college education, and which had changed him very little in his own eyes. He would have said that he was still "cowfolks" and thoroughly at home only in the cow country.

"I'm downright funny!" he told himself sardonically. "I'm damned if I see why a girl like that would look sideways at me more than once and yet I'm hoping that some sort of funny accident will happen; that Old Lady Luck will spill a girl into my arms. But a man like Kawrie has all the breaks with him.

"Young Lochinvar can ride out of the West all right, but he's got to ride East, where he's sort of a curious spectacle of Nature. Same thing when you swap ends — the Lochinvar who'd naturally be able to make his twine stick with a Western girl is the one who rides out of the East. Oh, hell!"

Footsteps outside the office door brought him back from these gloomy meditations. And interest in the coming interview with Mr. Norman Curtis, who, Pat had gathered, had much to say about the stage robbery, pushed aside other considerations. For just then Ross very much wished to lay hands upon something that would lead to the

criminals of Rayo County. He wanted to
end what had seemed to him mere ground-
breaking and foundation-building; wanted
to make an assault upon the entrenched
ranks of both the Ellard and Kawrie gangs.

Mr. Curtis was a city man. He said that
he was a capitalist, from Albany in New York
State, who had come West to determine
whether or not he would get into the cattle
business as the moneyed man. So Ross,
listening to Pat's account of this gentleman,
had wondered if perhaps Mr. Curtis were
not a veritable instrument of the fates, since
he seemed to have been highly interested in
the experience of turning his pockets inside
out before the gaping nozzle of a Colt and,
too, because he had no local connections to
seal his lips.

He came in, with Pat trailing. Ross stood
up and looked him over, impressed, in this
grim country of weather-beaten, silent men,
by Mr. Curtis's amazingly pink and cheerful face and the joy of living expressed in
his bright and twinkling blue eyes. Middle-
aged, he judged his visitor, beginning to
grow a trifle rounded in the midriff from
good living.

"Howdy!" Ross said. "I'm Sheriff Varney."

"Real pleasure to meet you, Mr. Sheriff!"
Curtis said smilingly. "As a matter of fact, I

find everything about this wonderful country a pleasure. But then, perhaps I have a peculiar idea of the elements of pleasure. Mr. Phelan tells me that you'd like to have my story of the stage robbery."

"Sit down," Ross invited him, kicking an empty cracker box toward Mr. Curtis and himself taking the end of the table. "I would like to hear all about the robbery. Don't know how much you know about conditions in this neck of the woods, but there were plenty of salty hairpins here before this robbery. Now, they tell me that a notorious bandit is operating in competition with the older settlers."

"El Tecolote — The Owl!" Curtis nodded, rolling the nickname on his tongue with obvious delight.

"El Tecolote," Ross agreed, moving not a muscle of his brown face as he met the inquiring eye of Pat Phelan from over the visitor's shoulder.

"Well, let's see. We left Vado in mid-afternoon. The driver was a chap named Fatty Trull and there was a shotgun guard named Morgan. Besides myself, the passengers were one Young, a long-legged cattle-buyer; a gambler whom the driver and guard called 'One-Card,' and a storekeeper of Rayo named Roundfield — four of us in all.

"We came pleasantly enough through the mesquite and the horses were making rather hard work of a long grade which the storekeeper told me is called Cerro Diablos, when I saw Morgan, the guard, lift his shotgun. I looked sideways and three men were coming out of the brush — all riding — on my side of the coach. They were masked with bandannas, all. But from the other side of the road came at that moment a cry of 'Tickle your ears, Morgan!' and with it, a shot. Morgan just slid to the ground. Two more men appeared.

" 'Now, Fatty,' the same voice said very calmly, 'don't you make the same mistake. Pull in those horses while we prospect our claim. It's common talk in Vado that you're taking up wealth sweated from the brows of the lowly wage-earners of the world to a soulless corporation — in brief, that you're packing five or six thousand to the Minas Grandes outfit. As crusaders against these unequal distributions of wealth, we have come to reapportion the said thousands.'

"Now, Mr. Varney, perhaps I'm not giving you word for word the bandit leader's speech, but it was exactly in that vein. I know it impressed me particularly as being the language, the turns of thought, to be expected in a man of more than usual education. And all of this — it came to me like a sledge-hammer blow — on top of the calm murder of Morgan, the shotgun guard. It typified the man who sat his horse beside the stage with a revolver in his hand, utterly callous in his disregard of that dead man. I tell you, I felt that I was in the presence of a devil!"

"You were!" Ross said grimly. "Indeed you were."

"He ordered us, with the same mocking word-play, to get down and enlighten his men concerning the contents of our pockets. While we were being searched by a squat black-haired fellow in overalls, who said nothing at all as he robbed us, I could hear other robbers getting the express box out of the boot and prying it open. Well, they certainly picked us clean! Money, watches, a big diamond ring from the gambler, even our pocket-knives.

" 'I have always disliked the vulgar ostentation displayed by certain members of your fraternity,' the tall leader told the gambler, One-Card. 'We take this ring to show our feeling in the matter — purely as a rebuke. I have heard of you anyway; there really should be a law against your dressing like a real gambler. Shaking dice with Mexicans out of tin horns is more suited to your talents than a gentleman's game!'

"They let us get back into the stage and told the driver to return to Vado — that being farther away than Rayo, I think. Young, the cattle-buyer, got off at a ranch, before we returned to Vado. He said that he had business in Rayo and would get a horse at this ranch. I came here on the stage the next day."

"And Young recognized this tall boss robber as El Tecolote, right off?" Ross frowned.

"I suppose so," Curtis nodded. "But he made no sign so long as the robbers were in sight. It was afterward that he told us that we had been held up by El Tecolote. He said that he had once had this outlaw pointed out to him in a Mexican village on the Rio Grande and knew his voice and figure."

"I'm afraid," Ross said slowly, "that your story, while it's interesting enough, is not going to help me a lot. I was hoping you'd have something definite enough to swear out a warrant on. I'm afraid, too, that Mr. Young is not quite what you'd call a dead-sure identifier. . . . You can write home that you got robbed all right, Mr. Curtis, but you can't tell the folks it was the famous El Tecolote that robbed you. Not and tell the truth, anyhow."

"You speak as if you knew," Curtis shrugged, with twinkling blue eyes steady upon Ross. "Who was it, then? That is, if you can properly tell me."

"That's the hell of the business," Ross exploded. "I know damn' well who it was. I would put the bracelets on him one-two-three, if I had a bit of evidence to take with us into court. But I haven't! Incidentally, did you happen to notice any other tall men in that gang?"

"One," Curtis nodded hopefully. "Very tall; very, very thin. He talked in a high nasal whine — a sort of sanctimonious, hypocritical voice."

"Oh-ho!" Ross nodded, and his eyes narrowed. "Not so good as evidence, but still the best yet. Reckon you could identify that fellow in a bunch of, say, fifty?"

"I think so. Yes, I'm sure I could. And, Mr. Varney, if you can produce him, I'll undertake to identify him by voice alone. I'll permit myself to be blindfolded while you have twenty men speak in turn. Then, if I do identify him and see that in height he also corresponds to that robber, I'll swear out a warrant and stick with you in the prosecution until we've convicted him or you tell me the task's hopeless!"

"Thanks!" Ross regarded the rotund pink-cheeked Easterner with new and more favorable expression. Apparently there was iron in that soft-seeming body.

"Four thousand they got, besides what they took from you passengers," he said to himself. "And they stripped you clean, you say? Even took your pocket-knives."

"Even my cigars!" Curtis smiled. "Not being posted on the etiquette of such affairs, but feeling very much in need of smoking, I asked the heavy-set man who had robbed us passengers for one of the cigars back. He laughed and refused, but rolled me a cigarette instead. And when I drew out of a little pocket they had overlooked my French cigar lighter, the leader told this other man to give me a match and take away my lighter."

"Life's a funny proposition," Ross said, regarding Pat with a rueful smile. "You come to a place and, all of a sudden, something you just threw away becomes valuable. You say to yourself, 'Now, if that's not hell!' But, as the Mex' have it — *es vida!* That's life! Here I had Keith Kawrie right in town, right in my hands. Now, when Mr. Curtis here is ready to swear out a warrant for him, we've got to ride to Rawles and likely smoke-up that bunch of prairie dogs to get him back."

"Kawrie! The tall, dark man you had the trouble with the city marshal about?" Curtis asked. "By jove! With a silk handkerchief across his face — Of course it was Kawrie! I'll gladly swear out a warrant, Mr. Varney! But have you any proof, other than my identification?"

"That and your identifying your cigar-lighter. Oh! You've another score against him, Mr. Curtis. In addition to robbing you, he's telling stories about you. He told me he got that lighter from a drummer over Vado way. Let's see now. . . . No-o, I reckon I'll just keep you as a witness. You sort of hang back in the timber until I bring Kawrie in. I'll get a bunch of John Doe warrants and drag Kawrie and Vic Lundy and Isidor Flint, and anybody else that's handy and then you can do the identifying."

"There were five of them in all. You account, with those names, for three. Then there was the chap who helped the extremely tall man with the money box — he was a man of middle height; walked like a young fellow; when he pushed back his hat for a minute I noticed that he had a particularly unruly mop of sandy hair. And a boy — one senses age by carriage, you know, even in a masked figure — with very expensive cowboy outfit, who held a pair of pearl-handled revolvers trained on the driver."

"No idea who that last one could've been," Ross lied calmly. "But maybe — just maybe — I know the sandy-haired one. I noticed him over in Rawles, when he was yowyowing about my shooting up a friend of his. Well —"

"Hey, Sheriff!" a man called from outside. "Got a fellow here that's trying to die on us. Can we bring him inside?"

"Good a place to die as any," Ross retorted. "Tote him in!"

He slipped from the table and moved swiftly to the door. A buckboard was coming swiftly along the street, followed by a good many men. It was a man on foot who had made the inquiry. He stood now, waiting for the buckboard's arrival.

"Who is it?" Ross demanded, frowning toward the buckboard and instinctively folding his arms. More trouble, he felt.

"Manager of the United Mines. Three hold-ups jumped into his office and killed his clerk and drilled him as full of holes as Ghost Mine Ledge, and that hogback looks like she'd had smallpox. No doctor out at the mine, so they carried him in to town and he come back to his senses and started yelling for to see you. So there's a doctor in the buckboard with him, patching him up

206

as he comes."

The buckboard halted at the office door and a limp figure was lifted and borne across the sidewalk and inside.

"Put him there on that empty cot!" Ross said, looking curiously at the square, tanned young face, now yellowed with the pallor of the near dead.

"I've given him a stimulant," the doctor grunted in a displeased tone. "He insists on talking to you. It may cost him his life, but I know him well enough not to argue; he's stubborner than a bronco mule."

"You fellows better clear out and let me talk to him, then," Ross suggested to the idlers who had trailed the buckboard.

They hesitated sulkily for a moment, but Pat Phelan, with the beginning of an unpleasant smile, moved toward them and they backed out. Ross bent over the still figure. The man seemed unconscious; his eyes were closed and his lips tightly clamped.

Chapter Nineteen

Ross's hand closed about the wounded man's. "All right!" he said gently. "This is the sheriff. Spill whatever you want to tell me."

The eyelids fluttered up and pain-darkened blue eyes searched Ross's face for a long minute. Then, "Bend over!" the man whispered. "Buckshot — and Talbot — recognized 'em both! Didn't know — other man. Talbot's mask — slipped. He knew — I knew him — That's why — he shot me. Buckshot — know those eyes anywhere!"

"Enough!" Ross cried. "Doc, give this fellow the whole course! You've got to save him, Doc. Now take him and do it."

He whirled upon Pat and the fascinated Norman Curtis. Pat lifted his brows.

"Could you hear him?"

"Talbot and Buckshot! What a name!" Curtis said. Pat, too, nodded.

"All right then! In case he dies, you're witnesses. Now the job is to gather 'em in. Maybe, Pat, oldtimer, this is going to be our last job, but *por dios!* I am going either to bring in those two murderers, or else — Well, you'd better stroll down the backs of the buildings to the Swan. I'll wander in the front. Doc!"

The doctor, an irascible-looking middle-aged man, lifted his head impatiently.

"Listen," Ross said in a low voice. "I want the word to go ahead of me down town that he didn't talk — couldn't talk. That you haven't got him back to his senses. Will you back me up?"

"You're the sheriff!" the doctor grunted without apparent interest. He bent again to his work on the patient.

"You fellows had better wander down town and let things get sort of quiet around here," Ross told the waiting group outside the door. "He's got something to tell me, it looks like — if the doctor can get him back to his senses. Looks like, though, he's gone for good."

They nodded and began to go back toward the center of town. And Ross was interested to observe that two or three seemed in more of a hurry to get back than any of the others.

"Good enough!" he said grimly to himself. "They wanted to know if he'd told me the names. . . . All right, Pat! Let's ramble!"

Going at a careless gait along the sidewalk, Ross thought suddenly of his old band, which had helped him in the war with Mig' Mora. A salty bunch! Every one a man to be depended on to the last cartridge and the last gasp of breath. He wished that he led them at this moment. But then, they should be coming soon. Tomorrow, even, might see them riding in — little "Canuck," lanky "Chickashaw," the "singin'est, shootin'est, shoutin'est cowboy on the river," as the others named him, fat "Hinky," whose fatness interfered not at all with the most uncannily accurate rifle shooting that Ross had ever seen, and "Big Llano," who never fought a man his own size — there being no others so small — and all the others of those who were not only his hired hands, but his friends.

Ross grinned to himself. I'm certainly lonesome! Wouldn't it be a lovely thing if a fellow could stake out an outfit up here and throw that bunch on to the range as riders, with Pat for foreman! But — what would a ranch amount to without Marie. . . . And that little damn' fool, Ed, he rode with Kawrie the other day. . . . Was a fellow ever up against a meaner proposition?

Abruptly he came back to the immediate present as he reached the Swan Saloon and saw, as usual, a knot of loafers upon the gallery. They regarded him curiously, but, he thought, without particular tension.

"Ellard around?" he asked the nearest man, and was answered with a shrug.

"Ain't seen Lake for a spell. Don't know, even, if he's in town right now."

"Either of his deputies inside or near about?"

"Maybe," the man shrugged again. "See Buckshot and Talbot arguing around, a spell back. Why'n't you look inside?"

"Thanks," Ross nodded and followed the suggestion.

He had two plans, one for dealing with the marshal, the other for handling the two alleged murderers, if the marshal were not in evidence. Either was merely the prelude to sudden action, he realized. This might well be the very last trail he would ever follow, for certainly he was thrusting his head into the lion's mouth when he came to take out of the enemy's stronghold two of the leaders of Lake Ellard's faction.

He had a sort of exaltation at this thought; it seemed to lift him above the ruck of humans in general; like one already dead, he could see from his height to distances that had been hidden from him before. Twice, now, Rayo and this job as sheriff had given him the experience that never comes to some men, and had never been his before. He went inside.

The long bar-room was crowded, as it was for twenty-four hours of every day of the week. A canopy of pale smoke from a hundred cigars and cigarettes clung to the ceiling. White-jacketed, pomaded bartenders served not only the stinging straight whisky that was the cow country's preference, but "fancy drinks" as well. There were all sorts and conditions of men among the customers lined along the bar and facing the gambling games in the adjoining room — visible through a great arched opening in the adobe wall.

Ross looked calmly about him. The only token of his mental state was the darkening of his blue eyes. Dusky violet they seemed as his glance roved about the room. He edged in to the bar and a man whom he jostled a little turned angrily but, with recognition of the tall figure, moved back courteously.

"Ellard around?" Ross asked a bartender who shook a drink for the jostled citizen.

"Haven't seen him, Sheriff," replied the drink dispenser, with show of politeness to equal that of the man Ross had jostled. "He hasn't been here since very early this morning — about breakfast time."

"His deputies, then?"

"I think they're bucking the tiger in the gambling room."

Ross nodded thanks and moved toward the archway. He could not see Pat in the rear, but it was typical of the perfect understanding existing between these two that he went toward the two killers, risking his life without thought on the perfect functioning of his contact with Pat.

He found the two he sought presently. But they were not bucking the game. Instead, they sat together in a far corner of the gambling room. Ross noted swiftly that on their left was a door that seemed to lead into a dusky back room. Buckshot's yellow eyes were like a watchful cougar's as he saw Ross. Talbot glanced up suspiciously as his companion nudged him almost imperceptibly. Each man sat with hands practically upon his guns.

"I just got word about this murder and robbery over at the United Mines," Ross said quietly, stopping before them. "Doctor brought the manager to my office."

"Heard he had something to say to you, but never come back to his senses," Buckshot nodded.

From his manner, one might have believed that he had not been knocked senseless and contemptuously tossed about by the sheriff.

"But he did get back his senses," Ross told him in tone hardly above a whisper. "And he told me he recognized the two murderers who killed his clerk."

If further evidence of guilt had been needed, the panic fear that showed instantly in the faces of these two supplied it. The yellow eyes of Buckshot dilated, contracted; his mouth sagged open so that yellowed teeth showed in a feline snarl. And in that instant the two of them, as if moved by one brain, went into furious action.

They had a small advantage, now, of Ross. He had been standing with hands at his sides while their fingers almost cuddled the stocks of their Colts. One or two players had been watching the conference curiously, but the bulk of those who played were intent upon their gambling. Nor had there been anything, to this moment, to arouse attention. So the speed of Ross's cross-armed draw had few witnesses.

Buckshot bore out that description of Yocum Nowle, who had called him second only to Lake Ellard at speed on the draw. He got his guns out as he came to his feet. Talbot was two seconds slower. A bullet from Buckshot's right-hand Colt sang over Ross's shoulder and smashed a huge crystal chandelier suspended from the ceiling down the room.

But at this pointblank range Ross could hardly miss, and he was in no state to be unnerved by missing the first shot. He had drawn both his weapons at almost the same time Buckshot's appeared. He stepped forward, further closing the distance between him and these two. Talbot died before he could fire a shot, torn almost to pieces by four heavy slugs that were so close together a man's hand could have covered them.

Buckshot fired only that one wild preliminary shot. Then he crumpled into the chair he had just got up from and sagged back in it, shot through the heart. He sat there with head drooped, chin upon chest.

Ross eyed them flashingly, then whirled to the gambling room. He had one cartridge left in one gun, two in the other. Men were apparently on the verge of drawing their weapons.

"Listen to me!" he cried abruptly, and his white face, his blazing eyes, seemed to put brakes upon their gun hands. "These two — and another — murdered the clerk at the United and probably killed the manager. But the manager recognized 'em both and they knew he did. That's why they shot him. I came in here to arrest 'em — but they didn't give me a chance. All I had to say to 'em was that the manager had recognized the robbers and had told me their names. They never asked what names! They just went for their guns. For they knew their ball of twine was wound up!"

Uncertainty showed in some of the faces; fear in others; but whether it was the proverbial calm before the storm, or whether he had shown them the futility of action in this case, Ross could not guess.

"I'm the Sheriff of Rayo County," he went on grimly. "I'd have just arrested 'em and let the law handle 'em. But they started this. Buckshot had his guns half out before I started to draw. Now, gentlemen, I certainly don't want more trouble over the matter, but if any man in this room goes for a gun, I'll surely try — and so will the deputies I've got scattered around before and behind you — to prove that it's bad medicine to monkey with a peace officer when he's executing a warrant!"

"Right!" came endorsement from the archway leading into the bar-room — a cheerful voice that drew the men's eyes automatically.

Ross looked with the others. With back to the thick adobe wall, with that double-barreled riot gun from the wall of the sheriff's office across his arm, with cheerful face pink of cheek and twinkling blue eyes, stood Mr. Norman Curtis. His attitude was that of the pleased spectator of a diverting theatrical performance, but the twin muzzles of the ten-gauge riot gun were steady as rocks.

"I'm certainly with you, Mr. Sheriff!" Curtis added cryptically.

"What's to do?" inquired another voice from Ross's rear, from the doorway in the back wall, which seemed to lead into a dusky room behind. "Sure, it was me that saw it all, and I'll be pleased to argue with anyone that disputes the sheriff's word."

His arms were folded — it was Pat — and over them showed the muzzle of his Colt. And in his small blue eyes was a war-flame. They were caught between two fires, these men of Ellard's in the gambling room. And, Ross noted with grim amusement, none of those in the bar-room did more than approach the archway which Curtis guarded. They kept at respectful distance and tried to see by craning their necks.

If further diversion were needed, Yocum Nowle's entry supplied it. He came like a furious, charging grizzly through the bar-room.

"Ross!" he roared. "Come out of this! I want to talk to you!"

Then he saw the dead men and his face mirrored savage satisfaction, which vanished, though, as if wiped out by stronger emotions.

"Come on!" he repeated. "If any of this scum here makes a move we'll salivate him! That's a good job you've done, but — come on outside!"

Ross nodded and moved toward him. So, in a compact little body, Curtis and Pat Phelan with them, they moved outside. Behind them was sullen silence.

"What's it?" Ross inquired curiously when he and Yocum Nowle had reached the sidewalk together. "I just dropped those two when they resisted arrest for murdering the clerk over at the United. They knew I had the goods on 'em and went for their guns. Ellard wasn't around, or there would have been more smoke."

"Good enough, but — where's my niece? Where's Marie?"

"Marie!" Ross cried, stopping short to gape at the big figure. "Marie! Why — why, she was at Mrs. Upson's yesterday. I saw her there. Talked to her a minute!"

"I know you did!" Nowle snapped impatiently. "She was supposed to come home yesterday, and when she didn't come I rode in this morning. Mrs. Upson, she says Marie was getting ready to come when a Mex' kid talked to her a little bit. Then Marie, she got on her horse and told Mrs. Upson she was going and, if I came in, to tell me she was coming home right soon."

"And she hasn't got there," Ross mumbled. "This is no country for a girl to be riding around over, by herself."

"Maybe I wouldn't think nothing much, if it hadn't been for that Mex' kid bringing her some sort of word," Nowle growled anxiously. "But — Ha! There's Mrs. Upson, and she's got the Mex' kid!"

Toward them came hurrying a large, square-faced and competent lady whose gray hair evidently marked no diminution of physical vigor, for she bore with her, his unwashed ear gripped firmly between thumb and forefinger, a Mexican boy of about fourteen.

"Well, I found him all right, Yocum!" she announced in a full voice, from perhaps fifty yards away. "And I shook the truth out of his lying carcass, I do believe! He was given two bits by a lanky hairpin named Briley Young to come to Marie and say that Keith Kawrie and Ed was waiting to see Marie outside town on that old Mex' trail that runs northwest past the Flying-X Ranch. That's all he knows, he says, and I do believe that if he'd had anything else in him I'd have shook it loose!"

"Kawrie!" Ross breathed in a dead, flat whisper. "Kawrie! Oh, my Lord!"

"And Ed!" Yocum Nowle's rugged face was white and murderous. "If that good-for-nothing boy of mine is tangled up in anything shady, by God, I'll strangle him

219

myself!"

"Never mind that!" Ross snarled. "I'm heading out that way right now! I was going to arrest Kawrie, anyhow, for sticking up the Vado stage and killing the shotgun guard. But now, I reckon, there'll be damn' little arresting done!"

And with that he left them at the run, to go racing down toward the corral behind the jail.

"Marie — gone to meet Kawrie!" he groaned to himself as he ran. "Gone to meet Kawrie. . . ."

CHAPTER TWENTY

"Not a track," Ross said in a low voice, more to himself than to Nowle, Pat, or the pink-faced Curtis, who had hired a livery nag and accompanied them.

They had come to a small knoll studded with loose rocks, where three horses had stood not long before among ocotillo and prickly pear. It formed a sort of natural lookout platform, upon the ancient Mexican trail that led vaguely northwest from Rayo, past the Flying-X headquarters ranch and on to the salt beds at the feet of the Pedros. Beyond here, as if swept by a broom, the ground showed nothing of hoofprints.

"They've headed for Rawles!" snarled Yocum Nowle. "What're we dilly-laddying about? Come on!"

"Wait a minute," Ross snapped. "I'm not so sure about that. And we've got no time to lose on sighting shots now. Figure it a little from Keith Kawrie's angle. Now, if you'd laid yourself liable to a rope around your neck, would you go hightailing it to where you could be found right off?"

"But, Ross!" Pat Phelan frowned thoughtfully. "Might he not believe, now, that he could be holding Rawles against the world? Would he be thinking, do you suppose, that we'd have many to lend us a hand?"

"I took that into consideration," Ross nodded. "But thirty-forty men'd be the most he could possibly pull in on his side, if he had all the time in the world! And time is what he never had. I believe he schemed this, he and that crooked cattle buyer, Young, in Rayo! It was — well, it was something that I'd said to him on the trail coming to the county seat that made him hit his lick now. There'd be nobody in Rawles but ten-fifteen men, and not that many if Vic Lundy had gone off on some job."

"Well, then," Nowle cried impatiently, "what's to do?"

"This! No telling what we have got ahead

of us, but one thing is certainly plain: Right now is the time the decent folks in Rayo County swing a loop over the outlaws and drag 'em to hell and gone! Now, one man more or less don't mean a thing to us here. So you, Nowle, ought to start rounding up the honest outfits, the ones you know you can count on for a clean-up. We'll go on to Rawles and see what we see. If they're mobilized, we'll drop back and wait for your posse. Anyhow your going won't change things a bit."

For a moment Nowle hesitated with stubborn face. Then he nodded unwillingly.

"I reckon you've got the right of it. Now, most of the outfits I want are to the east and south. I can't get to all of 'em, of course, but I'll send the word on, and it oughtn't to take more than a day to get together thirty-five to forty men we can bank on. I'll tell 'em to head for the N-Bar, and when enough come we'll be ready to hightail it any way you send word."

"Good enough!" Ross nodded, with eyes already lifting grimly toward Rawles. "I'll manage to send word. Now — *adios!*"

And with Pat and Curtis at his back, he spurred out across the broken hills toward Rawles.

Not much talk passed between the three

as they went on, now loping across a level, now foxtrotting over the broken lands to walk the animals up and down low hills. And from a hilltop they saw Rawles finally, and Ross drew glasses from his saddlebag.

"Looks quiet enough," he said when he lowered the binoculars. "Still — the mouth of a rattlesnake den often seems peaceful. But when you get in — Look here, Mr. Curtis, I certainly appreciate the way you backed our play in Rayo. But I'm telling you now that we're riding in where we maybe can't ride out, and I don't want to drag you, an outsider, into it. It's all right for Pat and me; partly, it's my job. I'm sheriff. But —"

"Let's go!" Curtis grinned. "I'm having the time of my life, Mr. Varney. And I'm absolutely a free agent. Nobody to worry if I get myself killed off. Still, I fought through a whole South American revolution not long ago and got out without a scratch. Perhaps I won't be merely 'among those present' if there's trouble!"

"Good enough!" Ross grinned, tight lipped. "No shooting unless they start it, or I give the word. Then, well — pop your whip and let your conscience be your guide!"

And they went swiftly down the slope, up

over a long, low ridge and into the single street of Rawles. As Ross had observed through the glasses, the town seemed empty. Here and there a cowboy showed in a saloon or gaming house doorway, but of the hard-faced townsmen he had seen on his previous visit, he could identify none. The men in Rawles today, he thought, were merely the wilder riders from neighborhood ranches, men who would not necessarily support Keith Kawrie in a battle with officers.

Again he swung down before the saloon in which he had bluffed Kawrie and Vic Lundy. With Pat and Curtis following, he clicked inside and up to the bar. Automatically, his eyes flashed to that corner where, upon the small box, he had seen Isidor Flint with his pious-looking *Decameron.* But the lanky hypocrite was not in evidence today.

"Where is Kawrie?" Ross inquired of the bartender, and that worthy shrugged.

"Now, you tell me and I'll tell you! Keith ain't been in since him and you dragged it out of here."

"Where is Vic, then — or Flint?"

"*Quién sabe,* Sheriff? She's more'n a mixologist can hope to do, keeping track of that bunch. And they don't tell me what they're figuring on, nohow."

With which final, very pointed remark the bartender looked thoughtfully up at the dingy ceiling and began to whistle as he polished a whisky glass. Ross paid for a round of drinks and remarked inwardly that the cheap whisky slid down like so much creek water. Grimmer and grimmer his face had become, with passing of the minutes here. Before his mind's eyes a picture persisted, for all that he shook his head as if by the physical gesture he could dislodge it.

Marie Nowle in Keith Kawrie's arms, with the grinning faces of Vic Lundy and Isidor Flint in the background. And, to make visualization the more maddening, sometimes the girl's face mirrored utter horror, while again she smiled up at Kawrie.

"Let's go!" he snarled to his companions, and sympathetically they nodded and trailed him outside.

From one saloon to another, until the last one had been inspected, Ross led the way, inquiring of each bartender in turn the whereabouts of Kawrie, Vic Lundy and Flint. In slightly varying form he received everywhere the same reply and sometimes, meeting a barely perceptible flash of mockery in the eyes of the one questioned, his fingers curled to claws, and he had to force himself to appearance of calmness; for the red murder impulse was rising steadily in him as time passed and clearer and clearer grew the details of that inner picture as it seemed to unroll before him.

The men who made Rawles their hangout during idle hours, as well as those who lived there under the rule of Keith Kawrie, were called hard cases without exception. But if any resented the grim contempt with which Ross eyed them today they managed to hide their emotions. Wherever they went, Ross marched straight ahead, turning aside for nobody; everywhere men stood back to let the trio through.

"Come on!" he snapped at last, when he had satisfied himself that none of those he sought were visible.

They went back to their horses and swung into the saddle. Curtis made a half-humorous grimace and grinned at Pat.

"I'm used to park paths and postage-stamp saddles," he grunted. "I'm beginning to see the why of a fixed seat and long stirrups — but education comes painfully."

Ross sat with reins gathered up, but with chin on breast. What to do now? How to find in all this wide, wild country the ones he sought? Suddenly Pat, whose eyes had been roving mechanically, clucked tongue against teeth.

"Somebody leaving town," he said in a low voice.

"I reckon we'll have to look into it," Ross replied in like tone, after an unobtrusive glance at the two figures who had suddenly appeared on the skyline of the Rayo trail. Evidently they had gained it from the rear of the buildings of the town.

So the three jogged at a running walk out of town and, once over a ridge, set in the spurs and raced across the flat until they had to climb the next ridge and once more become visible to the town. Another glimpse of the two riders going pretty swiftly. Over the ridge and again a racing, pounding gallop. But the next view of those they followed showed the pair turned west, off the trail and going faster. "Let's go!" Ross snapped and roweled his black.

They were perhaps two hundred yards behind the riders when one of the men looked back. For an instant the two reined in to stare. Ross lifted his hand in signal for them to halt, but the gesture was ignored. This alone seemed suspicious. Why should men leaving Rawles fear others coming from the same place? Why — if these two did not recognize their pursuers?

"Get 'em!" Ross yelled, and in the last yellow sunlight began a mad race.

But the horses ahead seemed fresher. Inch by inch, almost, they increased their lead. Then Curtis spurred furiously to come abreast of Ross. His blue eyes were glinting like ice.

"Can't we drop 'em? Their horses, anyway? I think I could get one."

"More than I could!" Ross confessed without slackening pace. "But if you want to try, ride off to one side and stop and crack down. But wait a minute! I've got to swear you in as a deputy first! Then it'll be legal for you to kill 'em, if you do!"

So, at the gallop, he appointed the New York man a deputy. Curtis spurred on with the last burst of speed the wearied livery stable nag had in him, then suddenly reined in and lifted the rifle from its saddle scabbard. Deliberately the muzzle came up while Ross and Pat swerved a little to the right and continued pursuit.

The rifle shot rang flatly. A puff of dust jumped at the heels of the fugitives' animals. Again it sounded, and a horse turned a somersault, hurling the rider out like a diver. The other man bent low over his saddle horn; his arm rose and fell madly as he quirted his mount. Twice more the rifle sounded from behind Ross and Pat before the hunched figure slid from the saddle with an arm raised as if in farewell.

Ross and Pat were abreast the man who had fallen from the dead horse. He lay motionless, face down in the yellow sand. They passed him and slid their mounts to a stop beside the second one. He had rolled face up and Ross, staring down, recognized a man he had seen several times around the saloon in Rawles while he had been with Keith Kawrie and Vic Lundy, a hard-faced little rider of indeterminate age.

"Too dead to skin!" Ross grunted without emotion, when he had swung down and examined the fellow. "Bullet snapped his spine and he never knew what hit him."

Pat rode over to where the man's horse had stopped with head down and sides heaving, and leaned from the saddle to scoop in the reins. They rode back to where Curtis stood beside his near exhausted mount, watching the other fallen one. Ross regarded the Easterner thoughtfully. He wondered what effect the killing would have on Curtis.

"Dead?" Curtis inquired quietly. "Thought so. Never knew a man to come out of a saddle that way unless he was. Yes, I've seen quite a few in my time, here and there about the world."

"That was certainly 'way up in high-class

Winchester-work!" Ross complimented him.

"I never could play the fiddle," Curtis shrugged, a thought grimly, "but rifle-shooting happens to be a specialty of mine. This fellow seems to be coming alive."

"He's one of your stage robbers," Ross remarked, stirring the sandy-haired one with a boot-toe. "When he gets some of that sand out of his ears, I think you'll recognize his mop."

"What happened?" whispered the sandy-haired one, rolling over and trying to prop himself up with his hands.

"I wanted to ask you if you still felt peevish about my drilling Swede Oll that time," Ross informed him gravely. "But you wouldn't stop, so I spoke to Mr. Curtis here about it. He thought the business over and told me he had an idea that you were a cowboy. He said if he wasn't mistaken, and you really were a cowboy, you wouldn't hanker to walk any. So if he stopped your horse, you see, you'd likely stop, too, and — he was right!"

"Well, you people got a hell of a crust, cracking down on fellows that're riding along on their own business!" cried the sandy-haired man. "Where's Lenny? He get away?"

"You might call it that" Ross shrugged.

"He went somewhere. What'd you hairpins hightail for? You know damn' well the sheriff's got a perfect right to stop anybody he wants to. And you knew mighty well who it was waving at you!"

The fellow was sitting up now, very sulky of face. His roving eyes found his dead horse, then, turning to the left, found Lenny's mount beside Pat's. Last, he saw the significantly sprawling figure.

CHAPTER TWENTY-ONE

The prisoner's tanned face twitched convulsively, then went gray. For the first time fear showed in his eyes. Ross seized the moment.

"Listen!" he snarled. "You'd better forget the monkey business! You're crowding the 'Pearly Gates Ajar' so close you ought to hear 'em quaking in the breeze! I'm hunting Keith Kawrie, and you're going to lead me to him! Now, spew it up. Where's Kawrie and the rest of the gang? What's coming off, that everybody's rattled their hocks out of Rawles?"

"I don't know a thing," the cowboy shrugged. "Wouldn't tell you if I did, but I don't know nothing. Me and Ed, we was going over to Vado."

Ross eyed the stubborn mouth with painful intentness. Feature by feature, he studied the beard-stubbled face, searching for every sign of weakness — and of strength. Then he turned to Pat and Curtis.

"I don't care how you feel about what I'm going to do. If you don't want to take a hand in it, that's all right. It's your privilege. But don't butt in. Put him on that spare horse, Pat, and tie his hands behind him."

"Now, listen!" the prisoner snarled. "You can't arrest —"

"Shut up!" Ross invited him, and for an instant his hard face and blazing eyes made the man step backward.

Pat deftly noosed his hands behind him and drew the rawhide tie-tie tight. Bodily he picked him up and lifted him up into the saddle of the dead man's horse. Ross, meanwhile, had taken down his lariat from the rope strap. When he turned, and the prisoner observed the sinister business with which Ross's hands were busied, he made a harsh choking sound in his throat.

"You — you're going to hang him?" Curtis inquired in a weak voice.

"I'm going to do just — that — thing!" Ross returned grimly. "Chances are, he's been buzzard bait a long time now. What's the difference, whether we give him the cottonwood prance right now, or wait a week? I did figure he might give me enough information to make it worth while to pack him along. But he hasn't done it. So he's just one of Kawrie's gang, and every last one of that pack is going to be wiped off the earth before I call it a day and a job! Bring him over to this cottonwood, Pat."

Pat, with face as grim as Ross's own, nodded and led the horse under the limb of the small cottonwood over which Ross had tossed the end of the lariat. Again the prisoner made that strangling sound, deep in his throat. Sweat was running down his tallow-hued face.

"Anything you want to say before we kick you over?" Ross inquired evenly, riding up alongside him.

"Wait a minute!" cried Norman Curtis. He spurred over, and the prisoner turned fearful yet hopeful eyes upon the pink-faced Easterner.

"Listen!" Curtis said to the prisoner. "Before you — go, would you mind giving me that belt of yours? It's the oddest one I ever saw, and I collect that sort of thing. There's nothing to be gained by burying it with you, and yet I would rather you gave it to me than to — just take it!"

"Never mind that!" Ross broke in roughly. "Lenny's getting way ahead of him. If you've got anything to say, say it!"

He dropped the noose over the sandy-haired one's neck and hauled in the slack viciously.

"Tie the end to that big root. It'll hold him all right. Ready!"

"Don't!" screamed the prisoner, as Ross lifted his quirt. "I'll tell you! I'll tell you! But you got to let me go! Keith Kawrie would cut my heart out. So'd Vic Lundy!"

"Ah, you don't know anything. You're just lying to save your neck!"

"I'm not! I was going to meet Keith and the gang."

With appearance of reluctance, Ross loosened the noose and lifted it off.

"Me and Lenny, we was dead drunk when word came yesterday for the gang to ride," the prisoner gasped. "Vic, he left word for us to come on when we sobered up. They're over at Caliente Canyon, this side of Vado, waiting for the biggest gold shipment of the year — forty thousand, I heard. And Keith Kawrie's got that girl of Nowle's. Isidor Flint's going to marry 'em!"

"Isidor Flint!" Ross repeated, hardly above a whisper. "He's no preacher!"

"Nah!" The prisoner shrugged. He seemed relieved now of his panic. "He's a damn' old scoundrel; the biggest drunkard and two-by-four thief and cutthroat Rawles ever see. But he can pass for a preacher where he ain't knowed. And they say that when the word came to him from Keith he grinned and patted that black book he's always reading.

" 'Got a ceremony to perform!' he told the outfit. 'Goin' to marry off a sweet little bride on this here holy book of mine!' "

"How many did Vic take to Caliente Canyon?" Ross snarled at him. "Quick! Don't yammer there all night!"

"About twelve — counting Ed Nowle and Vic himself. Now, you promised you'd let me go! Man, I got to hightail it clean out of this country. Keith and Vic would stake me out on an ant-hill if they knowed I squealed. Let me go an' I'll clean disappear in a mile-high cloud of dust. I'll run this goat here as far's the road's cut out!"

"When is that treasure-stage due?"

"Tomorrow around noon, I think. Now, that's all I know, Mister. I —"

"Who's Matt Sayer?" Ross snapped suddenly, on the impulse of the moment. "Sayer, the gunman? One that killed the man Baldy Fay?"

"You ain't double-crossing me, now? You're going to let me go?" the sandy-haired man said suspiciously. "All right, then!

That's Briley Young. When first he came up to Rawles he passed by that name, then changed his brand right sudden. He killed that fellow Fay for something or other at the Widow Serrano's roadhouse, east of Rawles. And he began to show lots of money right after, so I always figured he robbed Fay."

"Git!" Ross said grimly. "But what's your name, fellow? Lyss Burrell. All right! You had better make for Galveston or New Orleans, for we're going to publish how we found out about Kawrie today. And, too, you're escaping from the custody of the sheriff. You see, you're wanted for stage robbery, and if I hear about you being anywhere around this county after today I'm going to get you!"

But without a word Lyss Burrell drove in the rowels and sent his dead partner's horse to the eastward at a racing pace. Ross looked grimly after him for a moment, then softly beat his fist upon the saddle horn and sought counsel from the darkening sky. Neither Pat nor Curtis cared, after a glimpse of his face, to break in upon his meditations.

"N-Bar Ranch!" Ross cried abruptly. "We'll hit her through Rayo. It'd be plain suicide for the three of us to break in on that gang at Caliente Canyon. I would give most anything I ever hoped to own, Pat, for sight of our boys topping out of a draw right now!"

He kneed the black around and they moved through the twilight back to the Rayo trail, then turned toward the county seat. Ross rode in advance; Curtis and Pat Phelan came knee-to-knee behind him. Curtis looked thoughtfully at Pat.

"Do you know," he grunted, "when he made that hangman's knot and came toward Burrell he had me guessing. I didn't know whether he really meant to hang the rascal or not!"

Pat stared at the other through the growing dusk as they jogged the weary animals along. His small blue eyes were narrowed.

"I've knowed him since he was knee-high to a short Winchester," he remarked, and his tone was analytical. "Sure, I've seen him drunk, and I've seen him sober; I've worked and I've played with him. But in love — sure, this is a new one on me. You say he kept you guessing about what he was aiming to do? Well, my friend, I'll be telling you God's truth: Sure, I don't know *now* whether he'd have hung that fellow!"

And for the next three hours they went on, in a silence broken only by the faint jingle of bit and spur-chains and the mellow creak-creak of saddle leather, the horses jogging with heads down. Then the lights in Rayo glowed yellow in the valley below them and they rode on and along the main street, past the blazing halls and bagnios, to the sheriff's office in the jail.

"There's two-three horses in the corral," Ross grunted evenly as they swung down. "I guess they were Sheriff Troop's and his deputy's. Hope they're good ones; I hate to swap from my black, but he's too tuckered out to ride tonight."

"Sure, there's three," Pat reported, investigating the corral. "One apiece. That is," he amended with a grin, "if our friend here is feeling like more riding the night."

"Try keeping me here!" Curtis returned. "I'd go with you if I had to squat in the saddle like a Cossack!"

"What's that!" Ross grunted, turning suddenly toward the front of the jail.

"That" was the sound of advancing footsteps along a plank-floored veranda somewhere near by. Ross moved quietly around the building and Pat, with an oath, came swiftly past Curtis to follow. The Easterner, noting that Pat's gun hand had been quickly filled, himself got out his Colt and trotted on the deputy's heels.

Ross peered around the corner of the jail and saw four men, walking abreast, on the other side of the street, making no attempt at silence, their boot-heels thumping loudly on the boards. As he stared narrowly they came within the light of a Chinese restaurant and he saw Lake Ellard, the marshal, with a small, pale-faced man on his left. This one, in immaculate frock-coat and broad-brimmed hat, Ross recognized as one of the faro dealers in the Swan. The two men on Ellard's right were mere shapes.

The quartet, moving with appearance of grim purpose, came abreast the jail. For an instant, they paused on the edge of the veranda before the Chinaman's. Ross cast a flashing glance along the street, in the rear of Ellard and his companions. It struck him as an ominous sign that while men in plenty were visible between this and the center of Rayo, all were poised as if waiting, and keeping very close to the fronts of the buildings.

He stepped out from behind the corner and moved with deliberate, catlike steps to meet the marshal. Pat and Curtis followed, separating to move obliquely to positions just behind Ross and some four feet, respectively, to right and left of him.

"Something?" Ross inquired drawlingly

as, at sight of the three, Ellard and his backers stopped short, perhaps sixty feet away. He pushed back his hat, Ross, and stood with feet a little apart, balancing like a boxer ready to shift and strike.

"I've come to settle things once and for all," Ellard answered in a slow, deadly tone. "Since you hit town you've been right uppity and my patience is all worn out. Sneaking in when I wasn't around, and murdering my deputies just settled your hash. Now you can hand over your guns, you and that monkey-faced Mick behind you, or else —"

Inwardly Ross cursed his luck. Here, when he wanted most desperately to be riding the trail to the N-Bar, to Caliente Canyon, to Marie, he faced the possibility of death or a disabling wound. A showdown with Ellard had been on the cards from the very beginning. He had rather looked forward to it, as a hard part of his work to be fulfilled. But this was not the time he would have chosen.

"This is pretty unreasonable, Ellard," he said in a drawl to match the marshal's own. "I was just fixing to ride out on some mighty important business. Of course, I knew right well that you and I had a little talk coming, but this is a long way from the time I'd have picked. How about putting it off a couple of days?"

One of the men beside Ellard laughed outright.

"Yellow as a pesthouse flag!" he remarked clearly.

"What we waiting for?" snarled the faro dealer, and his slim hands curled and uncurled, curled and uncurled, sinister as writhing snakes in the half light.

"I figured you'd crawl at the showdown," Ellard told Ross. "But you don't pull none of that on me! The three of you — turn in your guns!"

Ross saw the hands of the four beginning to move upward. It was the showdown, and it was not to be avoided or delayed. His shoulder sagged slightly, and behind him he heard Pat whisper to Curtis.

"You asked for it!" Ross cried suddenly to Ellard. He whipped out both Colts.

Chapter Twenty-Two

What followed was like an explosion in the darkness, the yellow pencils of flame stab-stabbing, the steady reverberations like the roll of near-by thunder. Movements were automatic and stepped up to a terrific speed, impossible to follow with the eye.

Ellard's twin white-handled guns had come from their holsters in fashion to show

Ross how the marshal had gained his reputation. There was no opportunity here to try gauging his speed or comparing it. Twice Ross fired at the marshal, and at the same time let go with the left-hand gun without specific aim in the general direction of Ellard's companions. The four had stood with fronts enshadowed, with the light from the restaurant windows at their backs, giving them the semblance of black paper silhouettes.

A man swayed with the first roar of the shots — swayed like something wind moved, then crumpled to his knees. Ross felt a sharp blow like that of a glancing club upon his hat-rim. Dimly he caught the rattle of shots behind him. And, as in a dream, he watched Ellard crash face downward, and the figure of the faro dealer bend as to support the marshal; bend — but clear to the ground and without rising.

The four Ellard men then were flat in the sandy street. Ross jerked his head about. Pat was closing up, limping; Curtis lay still, with arm outflung. Ross moved forward cautiously, menacing the still group ahead with Colts that, he discovered only afterward, were empty.

Lake Ellard was dead; so was the faro dealer. One of the other gunmen was dying fast. The fourth breathed strongly, but had four bullet holes in his body above the waist. Ross looked quickly toward the Swan; men were beginning to edge away from the walls, to gather in compact little knots. That looked like danger brewing to Ross.

"Hit bad, Pat?" he grunted.

"Sure, she's nothing but a slug in my leg! But Curtis, I'm feared, is bad hurt!"

They went back to Curtis and found that he had been struck three times. Like Pat, he had a bullet through the calf of the leg and another had broken his gun arm, while the last had plowed through his breast high up under the right collarbone.

"Got to get him to a doctor!" Ross decided swiftly. "Let's carry him in, Pat!"

A rifle spoke metallically somewhere near the Swan. A bullet sputted viciously in the sand close by. Ross stooped and lifted Curtis, then ran for shelter, with Pat limping in his wake. They gained the office door in a rain of rifle bullets.

"This is the devil!" Ross growled. "We ought to be hightailing it, and now we've got to stick here and fight the damn' town."

Pat was flat on the floor peering around the door jamb, as he jerked shells from his belt and reloaded his Colt. He lifted the gun and watched, then suddenly jerked his head about with a grin.

"Sure, and there's someone of mind different from the others — more than one, begod! The omadhauns! They're being fired upon from beyond the Swan! They're taking cover like quail!"

Ross finished his labor of bandaging Curtis's wounds with the Easterner's own shirt. He came over to look. Men were scurrying inside the buildings; from windows and doors beyond came flashes of gunfire and, as Ross and Pat watched, running men dropped in the street before they could reach shelter.

"Now, that's right odd!" Ross remarked. "You'd think the town had two fighting parties. Wonder if Yocum Nowle could have come with his friends? They're firing both ways — at us and at those stores beyond — the Ellard gang is."

A man ran around the corner of the jail and was inside the door, stepping upon Pat's hand before they could straighten. Ross jerked up his Colt and let the hammer go. It clicked upon an empty shell, and the man cried out pantingly, "Friend, Sheriff! There's some of us in Rayo that's tired of Ellard and his damn' so-called Law and Order gang. Law and Order, hell! Law and murder, it's been! And so we been kind of sizing folks up and — and there's twenty-odd we can count on. When Ellard and them gunmen friends of his come up to murder you-all, we figured right now was the time to open the ball. Knowed we couldn't do nothing before you'd shot it out with Ellard, but we aimed to make him hard to catch after he'd downed you."

"What's happened now, then?" Ross inquired.

"Why, you kind of surprised us, getting that whole bunch. But not so much that we couldn't see the Ellard crowd getting ready to wipe out your chalk mark. So we opened up on 'em and before the sun's up tomorrow there's going to be some faces missing. I come up to tell you what's what, so we could sort of join hands and not be shooting each other. Our outfit's working around the other folks and they're going to get salivated proper!"

"Listen!" Ross snapped. "You're what I'd call a providential sending, you honest folks. Keep up the good work, but I've got to be hightailing it for the N-Bar. Got to pick up Yocum Nowle's posse and make it to Caliente Canyon. Keith Kawrie and his gang are there waiting for the treasure stage — and they've got Nowle's niece, too! If you folk'll keep things going with this gang, we'll smack Keith Kawrie good and proper. We'll make this county fit for a decent man to leave his pocket-book or his horse or his wife without a shotgun guard!"

"All right! Any of you get hurt in the battle?"

"Curtis, the Easterner that was with us. That's another thing: Get him to a doctor, will you? He's the saltiest New York Stater ever *you* saw, friend!"

"Who's that coming?" the townsman grunted suddenly, as the measured beat of hoofs came faintly from outside.

They gathered cautiously in the doorway and saw coming, from the direction of Vado, a compact group of horsemen, gigantic shadows in the gloom. Almost abreast the jail door the riders halted.

"There you are!" a voice announced triumphantly. "Rayo! Now, I don't never want to hear of you belly-achers telling *me* again that *I* can't smell whisky ten miles off! Llano! Canuck! That goes special for you-all. You been making impudent remarks all day. Now we've got to find old Ross —"

"Get down!" Ross called roughly, to hide the homesick pleasure he felt at sound of that familiar voice. "Chickashaw! Come on in — you're just in time!"

Pat Phelan, having directed the band to

the corral out of the line of fire and left "Monk" there for guard, came back inside and found that Ross had lighted an oil lamp. Chickashaw, faded blue eyes somewhat narrow as he studied Ross's haggard face, was making his brief report.

"And so we come fogging it. And we come early today to Vado. We never stopped and, outside town five-six miles, we run smack-dab on to twelve-fifteen men riding off from a robbed stage. They opened up on us and we let drive back at 'em. Finally they broke and run, with three pack mules in their midst. They left four men to check us while the others got well ahead. But, hell! Them gentlemen never met Winchester artists the like of Canuck and Hinky!

"We rolled up their bushwackers and left three of 'em dead. But the rest of the outfit had got tolerable far ahead. We being sort of new to this country, we 'lowed maybe we'd better come on in and wawa with you, Ross, and kind of see what's what."

"I wish you'd wiped 'em out to a man!" Ross told him grimly. "That was Keith Kawrie's Rawles men, and the treasure stage they waited for must have been a day ahead of time. These three you got — was one a tall, black-haired, good-looking hairpin on a buckskin?"

"Nary one! They was just three right hard-looking cases, but common cowpuncher kind. I see that fellow you mean, though, in the beginning. Him an' a heavy-set fellow was riding together."

"And — and" — Ross swallowed with effort — "and a girl? Was there a girl with 'em?"

"Gal?" Chickashaw repeated in amazement. "What'd a gal be doing with them holdup sharps? Nah, we never see none — and we see 'em close enough at first to see 'em all."

Ross was twisted by the twin emotions of relief and uncertainty. Perhaps, then, Keith Kawrie had sent Marie somewhere to await the robbery of the treasure stage. So she had not been in his hands, it might be. But, then, where was she now?

"You say you boys chased Kawrie's gang. Which way?"

"South and east. When first we sighted 'em, they was south of the stage road maybe a hundred yards and traveling east right along with it. Then we pushed 'em south, you see, maybe three-four miles. Then they turned east again."

Ross scowled, trying to guess it out from what he had seen and heard of that region. The Rayo man who had brought them word of the citizens' uprising now stepped into the breach; he was a storekeeper, Ross had learned.

"Easy as falling off a bucker!" he grunted. "Kawrie was heading for Rawles, round-about. Then these boys pushed him south and likely busted up his plan. He was figuring to just come around Rayo, I reckon, then go north to Rawles. Now he'll swing south past the N-Bar and then north again — unless, maybe, he was aiming to hole up at Deer Spring. . . ."

"Deer Spring!" Ross cried. "That's the old outlaw hangout!"

"Yeh, but they don't use it much since they can ride open in and out of towns right in the county. No use to stick way down there, where there's no liquor an' ladies; Rawles and Rayo suit 'em better."

"Well, anyhow, they're south and east of the N-Bar!" Ross shrugged. His eyes were flaming. "Come on, Chickashaw — all of you! You're a sheriff's posse and we're riding for the N-Bar. No matter if your horses are tired. We'll get fresh ones from Nowle. We'll gather up anybody that's come to Nowle's and land on Kawrie; then we'll drift back and help sweep up the pieces here."

He ran out to the corral, and behind him streamed from the door the compact band which had spread the terror of El Tecolote over a wide tier of northern Mexico before the death of Mig' Mora. And Chickashaw was crooning to himself as he went that last verse of *The Zebra Dun,* which runs:

There's one thing an' a shore thing
I've learned since I was born,
That every educated feller ain't a
Plumb greenhorn!

Southward they rode in Ross's wake, over the trail that had first brought him to Rayo. And to them it was as if no time had lapsed; they came with him as in the other days they had gone to strike at one of Mig' Mora's outposts, or the ranch of one of Mora's friends. Chickashaw was singing as he rode, breaking off now and then to curse without heat the weary horse that stumbled in the darkness.

"Damn' your wall eyes!" the even voice came to Ross and Pat. "Pick up your club-feet now, will you? Which you're a sight worse than Rowdy Hurd even, and that hairpin is awkwarder'n a cub bear a-cakewalking!"

"Sure, we'll be getting up in plenty time," Pat whispered consolingly to Ross. "What of Chickashaw — and sure he's the devil and all for an instrument of Providence, now ain't he! — stampeding 'em the way he done, there's been damn' little time for Kawrie to think of the girl. Don't you be worrying, Ross, old-timer! Not a little bit, even. Well — I wonder if our friend Mr. Briley Young-Matt Sayer, he's riding with the gang right now? That'll be handy, if he's with the rest of 'em."

Ross made no answer. Pat's consolations were well meant, but they could not reassure him. They had no power to erase a picture that had hung before his inner eye since the moment of Yocum Nowle's arrival in Rayo with word of Marie's disappearance.

He could hope that Isidor Flint had not performed a mock marriage, yet the fact that she had not been brought to Caliente Canyon strengthened that hope. But the picture which would not go from his mind, of Marie Nowle looking up at Keith Kawrie — and *smiling* — He swore under his breath and shook his head.

As he rode, he saw her vividly against the darkness that surrounded them. She was standing in the sheriff's office as on that first night of his in Rayo. Keith Kawrie had her hands and she looked up at the tall, handsome renegade. That night Ross had

251

thought that she was only half in earnest when she tried to pull away from Kawrie. She might be afraid of his influence upon her cousin, but she did not *dislike* Kawrie.

Something else troubled Ross. He slouched in the saddle and asked himself: "How will Marie Nowle look at El Tecolote the outlaw? What will she have to say to Tecolote?"

Chapter Twenty-Three

Midnight was long past; blacker, even, than before was the night that kept them shrouded. Somewhere close now must be the side road leading off to the N-Bar. Now there came faint sounds from ahead. Ross reined in, to listen. So did the others, and the horses milled a little in a close knot. For none there needed interpretation of those sounds. Somewhere ahead, heavy firing was under way.

"Come on!" Ross snapped, after an instant's wait. "Sounds like Kawrie finding some more inquisitive folks!"

They pushed the fagged animals forward with rowel and quirt and before them the chorus of the firing swelled until it was like the crackling of leaves in a flame.

Soon they could see the flashes in the

darkness. Again Ross reined in and stared.

"Sure and you'd say somebody had somebody else surrounded!" Pat remarked thoughtfully. "The question we'd best be asking, Ross, my son, is which might be who!"

"Stick here a minute with the boys, and I'll see if I can find out just that!"

And Ross moved on at a walk. There ran a series of flashes in a rude circle before him. A circle that closed in little individual rushes forward and inward, upon those who held somewhat higher ground. Softly, Sheriff Troop's rangy bay moved up nearer. He seemed well broken; the occasional bullet that sang away overhead or tossed up sand near his hoofs did not alarm him. Ross made for the point where someone was firing with care at the flashes uphill. Finally, he swung down and dropped the reins over the bay's head. He began to crawl up on that rifleman with all the silence and the skill of a stalking Apache.

At last he was near enough to separate a long bulk from the surrounding darkness on the ground. He poked his pistol muzzle into the man's back.

"Easy does it!" he admonished quietly. "Who are you? What're you shooting at?"

For an instant the man lay still, then

seemed to shrug.

"Right back at you!" he grunted. "Who the hell are you?"

Ross dug the muzzle menacingly into his spine.

"If there's any noise here, it might just as well be a pistol shot. Remember that! I'm Sheriff Varney. Now, spill it! What's this all about?"

"Hell! Then we're all right. I'm Anton Unit from the 7-Up, Justin Duarte's outfit. We got Keith Kawrie's gang on that little mesa; and, Sheriff, we're certainly fine-combing 'em! There's four of us, counting Duarte, from the 7-Up. Then there's Nowle and his five hands from the N-Bar and Old Man Engle and three 66 boys. Was four, but Engle and his gang was jumped by Kawrie tonight as they come toward the N-Bar. We heard the shooting and come out to see what's what. So we Injuned around Kawrie, and we're closing in on him right fast. Been fighting three hours now, I reckon."

"Where's Nowle?"

"Somewhere over to the left. Or he was when we throwed the loop around Keith Kawrie."

"There's twelve in my outfit. Pass the word along that I've come with a posse after Kawrie. I'm going to find Nowle now. I'll call up my boys and throw 'em in along with you. That'll kind of chink up any holes. How many you reckon Kawrie has got up there?"

"About ten, guessing by the firing. But we're whittling 'em down right steady."

Ross called to Pat, then went to Nowle and dropped down beside him, rifle in hand.

"Anything new?" he asked, when brief greetings had been exchanged.

"Nary thing!" returned the grizzled old rancher, and the word sounded like an oath. "If Ed was mixed up in this —"

"You don't know that he was. Likely Kawrie and Young just used his name for a stall, to toll Marie out of town."

He forbore to tell Nowle about the scheme for a mock marriage. The old man was troubled enough in mind, without having that to think of.

"Who're the fellows with you?" Nowle grunted, pumping his rifle clear after a swift shot at a flash uphill. "Got that devil, I reckon. Listen to him scream!"

"Old cowboys of mine," Ross said briefly. "Top hands, too, every one, any way you want to take 'em. I sent for 'em to sort of bolster up the hand of the decent folks in Rayo County. Well, I'm going to ooze around the edges a bit and see how things look. It'd be hell for any of 'em to get away."

He did not want any more questions from Yocum Nowle just then. He had told part-truth in saying that the band under Chickashaw were his father's old hands. Every one had been — but not all at the same time, nor at the moment he had set out to kill Mig' Mora. They had gathered around him from hundreds of miles of distance, for old Ross Varney had been the sort to make friends. But since Young, and others, perhaps, had been spreading tales of El Tecolote around Rayo, there was no telling what some answer of his might disclose. El Tecolote's identity was a thing which must be dealt with soon enough, anyway.

Cautiously, with lead from the besieged outlaws coming spitefully close as he went, he led the bay around the circle of besiegers, receiving now and then a word from one of them, or from his own men sandwiched between the cowmen. Engle, of the 66, an old-timer like Yocum Nowle, he found swearing tremendously from the pain of a shattered left hand and the loss of his Winchester, a bullet having caromed off the breech mechanism — the old man was left-handed — and put rifleman and weapon out of the fight temporarily.

"Man!" grunted one of the 66 cowboys joyfully. "You certainly could believe that he had took lessons, way he slings fancy cussin' around his head an' pops the tail off her!"

Ross watched the little dashes by which they were closing in upon the diminishing outlaw band. Then, as he came close to a shallow arroyo that seemed to run up toward the outlaw position, a sound from the brush below turned him about. He stood listening.

"It might have been some of the horses," he told himself doubtfully, when he heard no repetition of the noise. "But —"

He went noiselessly down the slight slope and threaded his way cautiously in and out among the mesquite and cactus. It was the black hour before the dawn and his progress was slow. At last he came to horses grazing, trailing their reins. Evidently the men at the N-Bar, alarmed by the shots exchanged between Engle's party and Kawrie's, had ridden up and merely hurled themselves from the saddle to join the battle, leaving the animals to take care of themselves.

"Somebody's coming!" Ross thought suddenly. Then, as he strained to hear, "No! Going!"

He had left the bay back at the arroyo. He scooped up the reins of the nearest horse and swung up. No time to call out to the others. Besides, this might be nothing much; some curious one drawing near, then retreating from, the scene of battle. If he yelled that somebody had escaped from the little mesa by way of that arroyo, it might disrupt the whole plan of battle; all hands might come running down, and so let those still hemmed in escape.

He pushed the horse forward quietly, in the direction from which had come the sound of those departing hoofs. Presently the animal slid down into an arroyo and here Ross felt safe to dismount and light a match. He went back and forth until at last he found hoof-prints. On the arroyo rim he sat for an instant studying the lie of the land from memory. On his right must be the rugged mass of the Deer Hills. Then, by following the line of these, he would come presently to a canyon mouth that was marked by the inward leaning of its walls that almost made an arch above it.

This was the dangerous trail to Deer Spring, five miles back in the mountains. The man heading for the spring followed the main canyon for a time, then climbed up a long, rock-strewn slope to a smaller canyon and on, thus, to the little meadow dotted with cottonwoods, where the never-failing spring made a tiny creek that disappeared within a hundred yards into a bottomless sink-hole.

"If Isidor Flint got penned up there on the mesa with 'em" — Ross studied his problem as he pushed on again — "then Kawrie has got her guarded somewhere and he'll just take her with him, not even pretending to marry her. . . . That is — But what's got me to believing that I'm on Kawrie's trail? Hell, this may be anybody; any of that gang would make a break for it if he could! But, if it's one that knows where Kawrie left her, that's just as good as having Kawrie ahead of me."

The sound of hoofs ahead was dead long since. Ross fancied that the rider had driven in the hooks when at a safe distance from the battle, and was racing onward now. So he ventured to set in the spurs himself and go at a lope.

There was the smell of dawn in the air and the faintest rose-flush in the eastern sky, when he came to the canyon mouth he sought. It was only a venture, a guess, but the best he could do. Deer Spring was a good place for such a hide-out as he felt Kawrie had planned. Whether Kawrie had used it or not, nothing but a visit would tell.

The way was rough up the canyon floored with loose stones on which the horse stumbled with a noise that made Ross swear nervously. To him it seemed that they should be heard for miles. Three miles, with the sky turning gray and the light making it easier to pick a path. There was the slope up which he must climb to make the side canyon's mouth.

It was a beautiful place for an ambush. One man among those boulders, in the mouth of that little canyon, could have held it against an army until his ammunition ran out. Ross jerked out both Colts and faced it. There was no sign of anyone awaiting him nor, in that welter of stones, any trace of hoofprints. He touched the horse with the spur and slowly they went up, stones rolling back under slipping hoofs, until at last Ross stared up the winding passage of the canyon. Nor had he seen or heard anything to indicate that he was not alone in all of it.

He hugged the walls going on, listening at each elbow of the crooked, roofless tunnel. But for all that, sight of the green meadow with its ruined stone cabin under the cottonwoods came abruptly. He had just time to see the cabin, the stooping figure, gaunt and black, before it, when from somewhere overhead a rifle banged!

CHAPTER TWENTY-FOUR

Something stung him like a wasp in the shoulder. He came sideways from the saddle, to go rolling over and over down a long slope, and lie still at the bottom of it, on top of the guns which he had loosed at the last minute of the descent. Blood ran down the front of his shirt, and beneath him, reddening his cheek where it touched the stony ground. And Keith Kawrie came running over, white teeth showing viciously beneath his mustache, rifle held shortened at his hip.

"And this," Kawrie said grimly, "is the end of the trail for the loud-talking sheriff of the many promises."

But only for a moment did he regard Ross's motionless figure. He glared back along the way Ross had come; back toward the main canyon. And now the gaunt figure at the stone cabin waved his long arm and yelled something. Kawrie made an impatient gesture. He stirred Ross contemptuously with his toe.

"Get our horses saddled, Isidor," he yelled. "I've just killed the Boy Sheriff! Hurry! I don't think he'd have come alone; somebody's following."

At which the mock-preacher leaped into

sudden activity. He ran around the corner of the stone house, snatching up two saddles as he went. And out of the cabin Marie Nowle came, almost as quickly as Isidor Flint had disappeared.

Kawrie watched her come. A sinister little smile lifted the corner of his mouth. He kept an eye upon Ross, also, and his rifle muzzle covered him still.

"Well, the run of the cards was in my favor, after all!" he said amusedly, when she had stopped to stare down at Ross's bloody face, the limp, sprawling way in which his body lay.

"You — you killed him!" she breathed. Kawrie shrugged.

"Well, in cases of this sort, where it's kill or be killed, I prefer not to be the one sacrificed, thanks! He came up here to kill me, if that were possible. So my shot, even though from ambush, was purely self-defense. I —"

But while she stared at him, the sound of hoofs came suddenly from down the canyon. Kawrie whirled about. His rifle muzzle twitched away from Ross to cover the trail. But abruptly the hoofbeats stopped and still nobody had come in sight on the trail that wound above the long slope at the bottom of which they stood.

"Now who —" Kawrie began frowningly. His black eyes were roving nervously from point to point of the canyon wall above.

Marie had not turned from Ross's still figure. She stared down at him, with under-lip between her teeth. She swayed a little. From behind them both came a sardonic drawling voice.

"I kind of thought you'd come up here, Keith."

Kawrie whirled about, but after a split-second of glaring, he laughed, a forced-seeming laugh.

"You certainly startled me, Vic. I had just downed our young friend and when I heard your horse I thought it must be some of his friends — that wild Irishman, probably. How did you get away?"

"Well," Vic said thoughtfully, coming up from the bushes on that side of the canyon, with a small grin upon his thick lips, "when I hightailed it, there was just four of the boys that hadn't gone over the hump. And one was shot through both legs, so there's just three that might've made the sneak with me. I looked around for you, but you'd rattled your hocks right smart awhile before. The others, they wouldn't come; they figured this was just a quicker way of getting wiped out."

"The fools!" Kawrie said quickly. "Why —"

"Now, if you'd showed us that arroyo when you found it yourself, chances are," Vic Lundy went on drawlingly, "we all could've made a break with some show of getting clear. But I always did suspicion, Keith, that when the showdown come you'd make out to save your own hide and be damned to everybody else. And now that I look it over, she looks to me like you *schemed* this from the beginning, to leave me and the boys holding the empty sack, while you hightailed out of the country with the gold we cached, and with this gal."

For an instant, Keith Kawrie seemed taken aback by his lieutenant's grim contempt — and Vic's clear reading of his plan. Then he laughed.

"What's the use of beating about the bush? With one small exception, I admit to planning just that. The exception being your own part in the plan. I started to tell you that heading the boys for Rawles was all a blind. But then I thought you might accidentally let it slip out. So I was going to send the boys on to Rawles and come here. Then I intended to send Isidor Flint over to get you quietly, so that we could leave the county together. It's about time. Things are getting too warm for us."

"You certainly are a downright sort of skunk!" Vic Lundy marveled. "Don't know as I ever seen a downrighter! And you ain't easy to faze, neither. You knowed mighty well I come up after you to put a .45 into your dirty head. But still you can stand up there and lie just as natural and smooth. You never aimed to give me a speck more'n the others. You was going to lift the gold and pack off this gal, here, and likely hit for back East somewheres and be a *gentleman!*"

"Why, Vic, old man!" Keith Kawrie cried indignantly. "Why —"

"Aw, shut up!" Vic Lundy snarled. His dark face was showing his bottled fury now. "Listen, you make me ashamed for the times I've killed skunks, while you was still cumbering up the ground. Now you been figuring you fell heir to the gold and the gal. Where do I come in?"

"On even terms, of course!" Kawrie said heartily. "Just as I said in the beginning. And the other boys are dead, so what's the use of bothering about them any more? Why can't we two act like sensible men?"

"What do you mean — even? What about the gal?"

"Well, of course, that's different," Kawrie said quickly. "She and I are to be married and —"

"We'll flip a dollar for her," Vic broke in stolidly, ignoring Kawrie's placating tone.

He turned his back on Kawrie, as if to produce something he wished concealed. Then he whirled back like a cat and jerked his low-hung guns. Kawrie had flipped up the Winchester with a tigerish grin of triumph. He died with Vic's twin bullets thudding through face and breast, still with that grin on his lips.

"I thought he'd try it," Vic nodded, with a grim smile of his own, shoving his Colts back into their holsters. "Well, honey, I reckon that leaves just two of us —"

But Marie had fainted. Vic looked down at her uncertainly, then took a half-step toward the stone cabin, where Flint had appeared leading three horses. But he whirled at the slight sound of Ross's rising.

"Well!" he cried. "I thought Keith said he downed you!"

"He thought he did," Ross said evenly. "But it was just a nice, bloody scratch. I was about to open up on him when you showed up — and beat me out of the job I've planned for a good while now. And now I'm here, I reckon all bets are off, Vic."

"Well, anyhow, they're kind of changed," Vic nodded thoughtfully. "You can *sabe*

266

why I aim to leave here right sudden; this here canyon's likely to fill up with too many folks to suit a peace-loving man like me."

"I reckon I'm a sort of amateur at this sheriffing," Ross drawled reflectively. "So, the way it looks to me, there's times when the law's good and times when just plain horse sense is better. Right now, it looks like horse sense to me to say to you — go on! Hightail it! That is, if you pass me your word you'll stay out of Rayo County hereafter."

"Why, that's right kind of you — and it's horse sense, too!" Vic nodded. "Tell you what! We'll work her thataway, *this* way: you got your guns? Yeh, I see you have. Well, go on and climb on to your horse and get back to the posse. You can fetch 'em back here, if you want to. For we'll be clean out of sight by that time. Now, that's fair enough, I figure. But, then, I always kind of liked your style since that day in Rawles. And if I had your luck, I'd never do a thing but bet on horse-races!"

"Then tell Isidor Flint to bring up Miss Nowle's horse. Then tell me how to get to the place where you *cached* the gold," Ross smiled pleasantly.

"Uh-uh! Uh-uh!" Vic grinned, shaking black head humorously. "That gold stays right

where it's — uh — buried. If I can't lift it some day, nobody will. And as for the gal, sonny, I'm afraid you're kind of young to go traipsing around riding herd on a good-looking woman. Me, I'll just have to stand your watch."

"In that case," Ross sighed, "I reckon the deal's off, Vic. I was trying to give you a chance, but if you won't take it —"

Vic, for all that he still grinned in friendliest manner at Ross, moved heavy shoulders suggestively. His stubby fingers curved a little, and stiffened; his elbows crept out from his sides. He was poised ready for a flashing draw.

"Now, sonny," he said good-humoredly, "don't you be playing the tom-fool. You ought to see, by now, that I don't want to have to down you. Don't go crowding me to where I got to. Do like I told you: climb on to that horse now and hightail it down the canyon."

"Can't be done," Ross drawled. "Grab a star, Vic; grab a star! You may pass for a gun expert up here, Vic, old-timer, but down where I come from — Did you ever hear of El Tecolote, Vic? Well —"

At the slap of Vic's hands upon Colt butts, Marie Nowle sat up swiftly and stared at them. Her lips parted as to scream, but she made no sound. With widened, horror-filled eyes, she watched the twinkling blur of movement. And it was upon Vic that her stare was riveted. For at mention of the name El Tecolote, he had gone for the guns that were almost beneath his hands.

Chapter Twenty-Five

Ross's left shoulder throbbed and stung. But he had achieved a calmness that kept the wound from influencing him. His right hand streaked across to the Colt butt on the left side. In a gesture that was like a backhand slap, he brought out the gun with its big hammer flashing back, to "slam up" on Vic. He heard as through a haze the returning roar of Vic's shots; felt the breath of bullets passing close. But the squat gunman dropped suddenly to his knees and let go his weapons, then fell face downward upon the ground.

Ross heard him mutter something as he snatched up Kawrie's Winchester and fired swiftly at Isidor Flint, who had clambered upon a horse and was hauling the animal around. He saw the gaunt hypocrite fall from the saddle at the fourth or fifth shot and himself dropped the rifle, hands shaking violently from the pain of the wrenched wound.

"Sure fooled me — that day — in Rawles —" Vic was mumbling. Then silence.

"Reckon it's about over," Ross said in a low voice. "Come away from here, Miss Nowle. Come up by the cabin. Folks'll be along pretty soon, I guess."

He moved that way, but staggered. Then a round young arm went around his waist and steadied him.

"Lean on me!" she said. "I'm — I'm not going to faint again. I am trying to think of — of all those as if they were dead snakes."

"It'll be all right in a minute," Ross said gruffly. "But when I grabbed that Winchester with my left hand it twisted my shoulder."

They went slowly down to the cabin. Flint was sitting up, whining dolefully. He had a broken arm and — that was all.

"You're a fine outlaw, you are!" Ross told him contemptuously. "Couldn't stick on a horse to make a run, just because of a broken arm. Well, you whitewashed scoundrel, that broken arm's going to cost you a broken neck!"

Flint seemed armored against that fear by the pain of his wound. He went on nursing the broken arm, rocking and whining where he sat upon the ground. Ross moved over to squat against the cabin wall and watch the canyon. Marie regarded him thoughtfully for a moment, then came to his side. He would not look up. He was thinking blackly that his job in Rayo County was done if Briley Young had been among the outlaws penned on the little mesa. And still —

That pleasant dream he had nursed in the beginning — of wiping out the outlaws and then coming to stand before this girl, much as she stood before him now — that was dead. He had been a fool to think that the reputation of El Tecolote, built of gossip from the deeds of every criminal between this and the River, could be slipped off. And when he told this girl that it was *he* whom the Mexicans first had given that nickname — well, that would be the end.

He pulled the walnut-handled Colts from their holsters and mechanically stared at the smooth butts; there was not a notch upon them. In the language of the cow country, he had "killed plenty." But, trying to look back upon the train of fighting in which lead had sung toward and from him, he could not think of an occasion when he would have, could have, held his fire.

He got up and went past without looking

at her. She turned to stare with vague puzzlement showing in narrowed eyes, as he set Isidor Flint's broken arm awkwardly with a couple of sticks, then tied his feet together. The drumming of hoofs down the canyon turned them both about to watch. Ross motioned for her to take shelter and obediently she moved into the cabin. He waited at the corner, then stepped out with Colts lifted.

It was Ed Nowle and his pale face was twisted with the fear of death. He flung up his hands with a gasping sound as Ross menaced him, then came sliding weakly out of the saddle, rolled over and sat up.

"You beat me!" he said. "Posse'll be along in twenty minutes. I'm the only one left of the gang. I made a break and grabbed a horse. But I never figured to find you blocking the trail here."

"Never noticed, either" — Ross moved, but to stand in the doorway of the cabin — "who else was blocking the road? Yes, Kawrie and Vic. Vic got Kawrie, then he wouldn't surrender and I had to down him. What's the matter? Make you sick? You and Flint — he's tied up, around on the other side — are about the weakest excuses for outlaws I've ever seen! Tell you what, Ed, there's *one* thing that today ought to teach you —

it's whole hog or none in this country! If you're going to swing the long rope, you've got to swing it! Otherwise, you'd better be honest!"

"Hell of a time to be telling me that now!" Ed shrugged. "I know I was a damn' fool, but Kawrie talked me into believing that this was the only life with any sense to it! I've found out a few things since then."

"Get on to that buckskin of Kawrie's, then," Ross snapped. "And fog it! Wait a minute! Did any of them recognize you when you broke through?"

"Don't think they had time," Ed said dully. He seemed unable to believe that he was being given a chance. "I sneaked down the arroyo to the brush and I was on a horse and a hundred yards away, lying flat on his neck, before they started after me. Then I played hide-and-seek and lost 'em for a spell. But they'll pick up my tracks pretty easy."

"Git!" Ross said. "Passing Flint — well, lie flat and go by fast. Keep your face out of sight."

And in a thunder of pounding hoofs, Ed Nowle vanished in the general direction of Oklahoma. Marie stared curiously up at Ross as he faced the inside of the cabin.

"Thanks!" she whispered. "Oh, thanks! It

would have broken Uncle Yocum's heart. I knew that Ed was running with Keith and I begged Keith to keep him from riding out on robberies. I — everything I've done was to keep Ed from being branded a criminal. That is" — she amended with a flush — "everything toward the last. There was a time when — when Keith Kawrie made me think him an unfortunate gentleman."

"All right! All right!" Ross grunted impatiently. "I wish your uncle'd get here."

"So do I," she nodded mechanically. Then, as if intuitively understanding his meaning and intention, she took a quick half-step toward him. "You — you aren't going to tell him — tell Uncle Yocum? Not — not about —"

"Ed?" he said with the faintest trace of a smile. "Why, the only thing I can tell your uncle about Ed is how I met him the other day when he'd made up his mind to try Oklahoma. And how, remembering that, I was so surprised to hear his name being used by Kawrie's messenger. And, of course, how Kawrie told me before he died — told Vic, that is, with me listening — about using Ed's name for a stall.

"As for that slick thief that slipped up and got away with Kawrie's buckskin while I was tying up my shoulder in the cabin here, a

274

while ago, I recognized him all right! He was one of the hard cases I saw in Rawles. Flint will back me up. He'd better!"

"That wasn't what I meant," she told him slowly. "I knew when you let Ed go as you did that you meant to keep his father in ignorance about his — his riding with Keith. But I meant — you aren't going to tell him that you're El Tecolote!"

For an instant he gaped at her amazedly. Then he recalled what he had said to Vic, while she lay senseless, or so he thought, at their feet. He shrugged dully.

"So you heard what I told Vic! Well, I don't know that it makes much difference. You — had to know sooner or later; not much later, either."

"Vic? I didn't hear you tell him anything. *I* have known about your being El Tecolote ever since that afternoon when we talked on Mrs. Upson's veranda. I — oh, after you left, it dawned upon me! Every time one of those horrible stories was told of El Tecolote, you always looked furious. And knowing that you were from that country; knowing, too, about your feud with the man Mora over your father's murder — why, I should have guessed it in the very beginning!"

"Well, then, that part's over and — I

reckon I'm glad. But I'll tell your uncle, too. Funny, isn't it? Law and Order coming to the toughest town and county in the Southwest through the terrible border outlaw; the fellow that goes around stealing women and shooting folks just to see 'em kick!"

He leaned moodily against the door opening and brought out tobacco and papers, making a fumbling job of cigarette building because of his stiffened left arm. But the lopsided smoke he rolled drew well enough.

He blew out smoke explosively. The sound was vicious as an oath. He stared down the canyon while she watched him with dark eyes unreadable, but with the tiniest of tremblings at the corners of her mouth.

He was silent for minutes, then, "El Tecolote — the Owl!" he burst out. "The deadliest killer the Border ever knew — so the Mexicans say. They named me the Owl because I rode into their towns at night and hit one of Mora's slinking killers and rode out again without being seen or heard — the way an owl kills a rat. And the name got to be the trademark for just any kind of job that anybody did on the River. Still —"

He shrugged and lifted his head a little, to let smoke drift upward in a hazy cloud that he followed with bitter eyes.

"I can't think of anything that I've ever

done, that I wouldn't do again in about the same way! Not a single thing! But some of those stories they tell about me, some of the jobs it's whispered I've done, they do rankle. I'd like to get hold of the men who told 'em. Everywhere I go, they follow me. Lies! Damn' lies! They put me in places where I never set foot. They have me doing things that no white man would think of doing."

"And now?" she asked him, very softly.

"Now?" he repeated savagely. "Now — Let me tell you something: I came up here to kill the man who killed a friend of mine. You know that. You know that I came looking for Matt Sayer. But there was really more than that, in my mind. I kept wondering as I rode the trail if there might not be a chance up here, away from the River and all the old things. A chance to start out all over again. Ross Varney and El Tecolote are not coupled in people's minds, even on the Border. That's why I've used my own name in Rayo. I thought that maybe I could let El Tecolote die — get to be one of those stories the *vaqueros* tell by the camp fire. After a while, after you-all had made me sheriff, I wanted that more than ever. There was a particular reason — you know that, too. But now —"

He flipped away the butt of his cigarette.

He turned with small shoulder movement to face her.

"*La casa sueña* — the house of dreams. . . . That's what I built. And now I have to say good-by to it. I don't know whether it had more of hurt to it, or pleasure. But either way the house has tumbled down. There's nothing left that I can see, but the long, long road away from it. So —"

"Have you ever been up on Perro Creek?" she asked him with a quick irrelevance that jerked him from his own gloomy thoughts. "It's north of the N-Bar," she explained, when he shook his head slowly, and frowned. "A lovely creek. . . ."

"No, I don't know it. And where I'm going, chances are I'll never see it, or any of the other range around here that I haven't already seen. But what made you mention it?"

"It's Uncle Yocum. He's always talking about Perro Creek, and wishing he were twenty-five years younger. He says it's a natural cow range and pretty soon someone's going to buy it up dirt-cheap and make a fortune if and when he sells it. So he's been talking about pushing north and taking it."

"Oh," Ross nodded, indifference replacing puzzlement on his face. "I see. Well —"

"The man who takes it up now must be strong enough to hold his own against rustlers. Uncle Yocum is too old for that sort of thing. Besides, he has all the range he can handle now, with Ed gone. My idea is that he would better buy the Perro Creek country and sell it, with a stocker-herd, to some enterprising young man. He can afford to do it on easy terms. And it oughtn't to be hard to find the right young man — some ex-sheriff, say. . . ."

Bewildered again, he stared at her. She faced him very gravely. He shook his head.

"It sounds interesting. Everything you say is sensible. But I swear I don't add it all up and make anything out of it that seems to bear on — well, all this around us. On me!"

"You don't? I said 'some ex-sheriff.' . . ."

And gravity vanished. She smiled at him.

"Marie!" he said very slowly. "You — I'm thick-headed, I guess, else you're forgetting the name they gave me —"

"I'm afraid it should have been Tonto — Stupid!" she said, and laughed. "Don't you know that *I* know you didn't go around stealing girls, doing all the other things that Briley Young said you did? I'm sorry about all that, down on the Border; I'm sorry, that circumstances made you a gunman. But I'm as much a part of this country as you are; I know what a man faces and what he'll go on facing for years to come. I'm sorry about it all, but I can put it out of mind."

She stopped, looking up at him.

"If you can," she said softly, "will you — try?"

He put out both hands, caught her arms and drew her to him. In the curve of his arm she tilted her head, lifting her face. He bent to her mouth and her arms came up around his neck. Minutes later he led her over to the corner of the ruined cabin that was farthest from the whines of Isidor Flint. There was a cottonwood log there. They sat down on it and she put her dark head down upon the rough flannel of his shirt.

"La casa sueña," she said slowly. "The Dream House. . . . I like that name. When we build a big rambling adobe ranch-house on Perro Knoll, with big cottonwoods all around it, and irrigation ditches watering my flower-beds and your alfalfa and corn-fields, we'll call it Casa Sueña. And you'll be United States Senator after a while —"

He tightened his arm around her and lifted her chin with his hand to kiss her. The tension of days past had gone. He rubbed bearded chin against her cheek. She straightened suddenly.

"I told you that I didn't believe the story

about your stealing that cow-trader's new wife, Ross —"

"Why didn't you? Who told you about it — told you that I didn't, I mean? Did Pat Phelan —"

"Nobody told me. I never asked. I just knew it wasn't so because I'd come to know a good deal about you. And because — well, I suppose because I didn't want to believe it! But what did happen?"

"That is something you'll never know," he grinned. "The beginning of the perfect trust that every wife should have in her husband. We'll even forget that you ever asked me. It evens us, too, for the way you made up to Kawrie, holding hands with him, wondering if it wouldn't be fine to go East with him and be Mrs. Keith Kawrie — or whatever his name was. Anyway —"

Hoofbeats sounded, coming up the canyon. Ross lifted his head, watching. A bunch of riders were rounding the elbow, Yocum Nowle in the van. Yocum Nowle, who was going to be robbed at one stroke of the beautiful Perro Creek range and his housekeeper.

He lifted his hand to Ross, who went forward to meet him. Nowle looked down with grim preoccupation, jerked his grizzled head to indicate the canyon behind him.

"Looks like Rayo County's so clean-swept we can heave away the broom," he drawled. "You found Marie all right. But Ed —"

"But Ed's all right too. I'll tell you that story after a while. Right now I want to talk about the sheriff job, and the quickest way of resigning out of it, and getting into the cow business, and things like that."

Yocum Nowle stared at him. Then, instinctively it seemed, his eyes lifted to where Marie was coming from the cabin toward them. He looked at her, then at Ross.

"Oh!" he said. "Oh! Well, a lot of good sheriffs have gone that road. I reckon you're no better than they was."

We hope you have enjoyed this Large Print book. Other Thorndike, Wheeler, and Chivers Press Large Print books are available at your library or directly from the publishers.

For information about current and upcoming titles, please call or write, without obligation, to:

Publisher
Thorndike Press
295 Kennedy Memorial Drive
Waterville, ME 04901
Tel. (800) 223-1244

or visit our Web site at:

http://gale.cengage.com/thorndike

OR

Chivers Large Print
published by BBC Audiobooks Ltd
St James House, The Square
Lower Bristol Road
Bath BA2 3SB
England
Tel. +44(0) 800 136919
email: bbcaudiobooks@bbc.co.uk
www.bbcaudiobooks.co.uk

All our Large Print titles are designed for easy reading, and all our books are made to last.